STOLEN PONIES

Christine Pullein-Thompson

CAVALIER
PAPERBACKS

© Christine Pullein-Thompson 1994

Published by Cavalier Paperbacks 1994
PO Box 1821, Warminster, Wilts BA12 0YD

Cover Design by Michelle Bellfield
Cover Photograph by Alistair Fyfe
Courtesy of The Infantry Saddle Club, Warminster

ISBN 0–899470–01–8

Typeset in New Century Schoolbook and Ottawa
by Ann Buchan (Typesetters), Shepperton
Printed and bound by
Cox and Wyman, Reading, Berkshire

CHAPTER ONE

They were ready. They mounted and rode out of their stable yard, along the street, past the station; there was a breeze in their faces, which to Joanna seemed to smell already of the moors, of bracken and heather, peat and bog.

Anthony was thinking, this time next year I shall be in the army, this is my last summer on the moors. He was holding each moment in his hand; it seemed his last summer without responsibilities, next year he might be anywhere—Cyprus, Germany, the Falklands.

To Carol it was simply the beginning of the holidays, of the longest and best holidays of all, of the summer holidays. Her heart was singing as they left the town behind and could see the hills and moors already in the distance, purple, grey-green and brown. Her pony, Ninepin, jogged, shying at the lorries, tossing his head, anxious to keep ahead of Joanna's long-necked black, Mulberry, and Anthony's fifteen hand Intruder. They made a fine clatter as they rode through the little town and people seeing them said, "There go the Richardsons to their cottage for the summer."

"I hope Mum remembers the bag of things we left in the saddle-room," said Joanna. And she wondering whether Sylvie would be a nuisance, remembering the French girl who had come to stay with them for

3

the summer, who couldn't understand their preoccupation with riding, who wanted to go to night clubs.

"Ninepin knows where he's going, I know he does," cried Carol. "Look how cheerful he is!"

"Intruder does, too. He feels quite different," Anthony said.

There was a family resemblance between them; yet they weren't really alike: Joanna had her mother's aquiline nose, blue grey eyes, a broad brow. She was slow to anger, but when roused would resort to biting sarcasm. Anthony was altogether kinder, brown-eyed, dark haired with a gentle mouth, and nose which was squashy; he was shorter than Joanna with broad shoulders.

Carol, the youngest, had nut-brown hair, blue eyes, the same nose as Joanna; she was small for her age, light and tireless. Anthony was nearly seventeen, Joanna fourteen, Carol ten. They had been to the cottage every summer for as long as they could remember. The only difference was that this was Anthony's last summer, and this year they had Sylvie too, who was unpredictable and liable to yearn for the cinema, and teenagers more exciting than the Richardsons to go to the night club with.

"I wonder whether there'll be lots of foals on the moors this year," Joanna said, and saw them with their mothers, long-legged fluffy, with bright eyes.

They left the town behind. The road ahead was straight, but presently it would start winding round valleys and gullies like a foreign road, until finally they left it and climbed the stony path to the cottage which gazed down bracken-covered slopes to the River Flowe.

Mrs Richardson would arrive before them in the Ford Escort, later their father would join them from

4

his office in his Golf. The arrangement had been the same for years, only the cars had changed, become newer and better as the business had prospered.

The cottage had a small stable and a rough paddock at the back. There was a garage for two cars at the bottom of the path. There was no electricity; they cooked by gas which was held in containers and went to bed by candlelight.

Joanna thought of that as they began to trot. How will Sylvie like it? she wondered. I wish now she had never been invited. I don't particularly want to stay with her next Easter even if it does improve my French, she thought.

"Don't you think Sylvie's going to hate it?" she asked her brother.

"I don't see why."

"But what will she do? There's nothing for her to do," replied Joanna.

"She'll find something," Anthony replied.

"She can embroider. She likes sewing, doesn't she?" called Carol who was ahead of them all, tearing along the road.

"Steady. What's the hurry?" shouted Anthony.

"It's Ninepin. He wants to get to the moors," called Carol.

If only Sylvie liked riding, thought Joanna.

I hope lots of things happen this time, nothing much happened last year, remembered Carol: Dad fished and we all rode, and we went to the sea twice, and tamed the wild ponies, and went up and down to the farm fetching milk and things, and Ninepin lost his shoe on the second day and Joanna fell off and concussed herself. If Sylvie's tiresome, I shall pack myself a picnic lunch every day and disappear.

They rode on and on each in his own private world,

each imagining the weeks ahead, none of them guessing that ahead of them lay the most exciting summer of them all.

The O'Connors were ready; they stood around the caravan chattering like magpies. On each side of them grey houses, four stories, reached towards the sky.

"All set? All aboard the lugger and the girl is mine," quoted Mr O'Connor.

We're going, sang Sean's heart.

"Come on," cried Maggie, calling to their smooth-coated terrier. "Come on, Nipper, or you'll be left behind."

"He'll come all right," said Mrs O'Connor.

Where shall we stop to-night? wondered Maggie, and saw hills soft and tranquil beneath a rising moon.

They climbed into their battered Vauxhall Astra.

"We're off," cried Mrs O'Connor, starting the engine.

"Sit still. Don't scramble so," said Mrs O'Connor to the youngest of the family, Richard.

Sean was twelve, dark, blue-eyed; charming, slap-dash, he was guided by impulse. He started to sing now, an old Irish song he had heard as a tiny boy when they still lived in Ireland. Richard was fair like his mother with grey-green eyes. Two years old, he sat between his parents gazing out of the window and mouthing non-existent words.

Maggie had the same colouring as Sean, but she wore her hair in a curly fringe and was thoughtful, uncritical and generous. Now she was thinking, there'll be ponies on the moors, remembering the Connemaras which had grazed outside their cottage in Ireland.

Last summer they had spent their holiday on a farm. There had been ponies, and she and Sean had ridden nearly every day; they had spent all their savings, but during the last year they had saved again and Maggie now had two ten pounds in the pocket of her jeans.

Every few moments she felt her pocket to make sure they were still there. She was fourteen and a half. She sat in the back of the car with Sean and Nipper, and every few moments the little dog licked her face.

Mrs O'Connor was fat and kind, the sort of person who laughs till she cries. Her husband was tall and unpredictable with a crop of wild black hair. One week he would be laughing and the next sunk in the deepest gloom.

But as they drove out of the dirty city through trim suburbs of new houses, they were all merry. Around them, birds were singing in clipped hedges and orderly trees; grass verges appeared vivid in the sunlight; as they travelled farther and farther from the city, houses grew fewer until they were really in the country with cows cropping dry August grass, corn standing golden, acre upon acre.

One day I shall live in the country, decided Maggie, in a little white farmhouse surrounded by tumbling fields. There'll be loose-boxes and Jerseys, with placid eyes, and my very own horse, which will be grey and called Kilkenny.

I shall rear the geese and milk the cows, and ride, and pick the apples in the orchard and 'Live alone in the bee-loud glade', she decided, remembering Yeats' poem because like most of the Irish she knew a great deal of poetry.

I hope we stop somewhere between the moors and

the sea, Sean was thinking, and he saw rocks slippery with seaweed, felt sand under his feet, and the rush of the sea against him as he waded in to swim.

Richard went on talking and gurgling to himself. Mrs O'Connor commented on the landscape.

"Must be cold here in winter; all right at this time of year," she said and "That cottage could do with a new roof. Proper Irish it looks to me."

She had never liked the country. "Give me the town any day," she would say. "Plenty going on all the time. The country's all very well for holidays . . ."

Mr O'Connor drove steadily on in silence, his eyes drinking the beauty of the landscape, nostalgic suddenly for Ireland, wondering whether they would ever go back.

They stopped on the edge of a wood for lunch. They ate sausages out of a tin, new bread, bananas, apples, biscuits. They drank tea, except for Richard, who had orange juice. They climbed back into the car and drove on through towns and villages, and country which became rougher until at last they could see the moors, grey, purple, green and brown in the distance.

"Look, look!" they shrieked then.

"Moors, oh look at the moors,"cried Mollly.

"Do you think the sea's on the other side?" asked Sean.

"Hills, hills, look," Mrs O'Connor commanded Richard, holding him up so that he could see out of the window. "Hills", he repeated. "That's right. Hills," said Mrs O'Connor.

"That's Longmoor," said Mr O'Connor. We're stopping somewhere there, at a farm I was told about."

A little farm among the moors, thought Maggie.

"There are wild ponies, aren't there?" asked Sean.

"Lots and lots of them," replied Mr O'Connor.

"Oh, Richard, and all down my dress. He's been sick. Must be excitement," said Mrs O'Connor.

They mopped up Richard, and Mrs O'Connor's flowered print dress. They drove on, and every moment the scenery became wilder and the road more twisty until they were driving round valleys and deep gullies, and then between wooded hills which reached right down to the road. And now twilight was stealing across the moors and there was a red sun, which touched the hills with red and gold. The beauty of it all seemed to sink right into Maggie's being, and Sean kept saying, "Isn't the sunset great? I didn't know the moors would be like this," And Richard slept on his mother's lap, while Mr O'Connor drove, still remembering Ireland.

Presently they passed the Richardsons hacking through the twilight to their cottage.

"Look, look, horses," said Maggie.

"Ssh, you'll wake Richard," hushed Mrs O'Connor.

"There are three of them," said Sean. "A bay, a black and a chestnut."

I hope we can ride, thought Maggie, and saw herself meeting the sunset, a lone figure on a horse, red and gold.

"Well, do you think you'll like Longmoor?" asked Mr O'Connor.

"Yes," cried Sean and Maggie, waking Richard, exciting Nipper who started to yap, making Joanna turn to Anthony and exclaim, "Gosh, the people in that car are making a row,"

"Beastly tourists," exclaimed Carol. "I bet they leave paper everywhere."

CHAPTER TWO

The Richardsons dismounted outside the cottage.

"Whew. I'm stiff!" exclaimed Joanna with a grimace.

"Ninepin's so pleased to be here. Aren't you?" Carol asked her pony.

It looks just the same, thought Anthony, gazing at the wooden cottage, which was shaped like an L, and stood alone at the end of the path with only the moors behind.

Mrs Richardson came out to greet them.

"Did you have a good ride?" she asked. "This place is full of cobwebs. Hurry up and come and help."

In appearance she resembled Joanna, but she, like Carol, had an endless store of energy. Sometimes she felt that without her the Richardsons would do nothing.

"Daddy isn't here yet then?" asked Anthony.

"No, he'll be late, He had a board meeting. Hurry," replied Mrs Richardson.

"Where's Sylvie?" asked Joanna as they took off their saddles.

"She's taken the dogs for a walk. Do get a move on," said Mrs Richardson.

They turned out their ponies and watched them roll. The sunset had gone; instead a moon shimmered among stars, giving the moors a mystic quality.

They stood and smelt the air. They could see Sylvie returning with the dogs and Carol waved. From the cottage their mother called, "Come on, there's lots to be done."

"It's wonderful to be here again," exclaimed Anthony.

"Hello. Did you see the sunset? It was pretty , was it not—so much colour, like a painting," called Sylvie gesticulating, small and foreign in the moonlight.

They all went in together. Mrs Richardson was opening tins. "Tomato soup, scrambled eggs and peas, pineapple chunks. Will that do?" she asked.

Except for Sylvie, they all said yes; she, typically French, decided Carol, wanted an omelette, but was overruled by the Richardsons, who insisted that scrambled eggs was the traditional dish of arrival.

Mr Richardson arrived and asked, "All got here all right, then?" He was large, with grey hair and steady blue eyes. He liked hunting, shooting and fishing and was equally liked and hated by the local sportsmen.

They all sat down at the table in the small kitchen and started to swallow soup.

"By the way, do you know there is a caravan parked in the orchard at the farm? Seems to be a whole family there, and a wretched little dog which chased my cat."

"Oh no, not really," exclaimed Mrs Richardson.

"Don't say people are going to start coming to Longmoor. That would be the end," said Joanna.

"It'll be campers next," said Anthony.

"It must be the people we passed. Perhaps they're nice if they've got a dog," suggested Carol.

"Perhaps they'll become friends. It's nice to have friends, is it not?" inquired Sylvie rather uncertainly.

"They may not come up here. They may spend their time at the sea," said Joanna hopefully.

"I don't suppose they'll bother us," said Mr Richardson. "By the way, I stopped and had a word with Mr Wells at The Crown. Apparently there's

11

something funny happening to the ponies. They keep disappearing. People are getting rather alarmed."

"Disappearing?" said Carol.

"What happens to them?" asked Joanna.

"Have they called in the police?" inquired Anthony.

"Isn't anyone doing anything?" demanded Mrs Richardson.

"Well it's only just started apparently."

"How awful," exclaimed Joanna.

"But why should they disappear?" asked Sylvie.

"That's what everybody wants to know," said Mr Richardson.

"Somebody must be stealing them for meat," cried Carol.

"Don't. We're eating," said Mrs Richardson.

"I don't want to eat any more," cried Carol, pushing away her soup.

Joanna was glad that scrambled eggs followed the soup; any meat now would be suspect as far as she was concerned.

"We eat plenty of horse meat in France; but here. . . I didn't think you eat horses here," said Sylvie.

"Our dogs do," said Joanna.

"In the war foals were passed off as veal," said Mr Richardson.

"It's foul," cried Carol. "We must do something about it."

"We'll dedicate our holiday to it," said Anthony.

Joanna, Anthony and Carol looked at one another and knew then that between themselves they had taken a silent oath to devote their holidays to solving the mystery. From now on nothing else would matter. Already the O'Connors were forgotten as they cleared away the soup bowls and started to eat scrambled eggs.

"I suppose they shoot them," exclaimed Joanna.

"Or lasso them," suggested Carol.

"No-one seems to have heard any shots," said Mr Richardson.

"It's all rather gruesome, isn't it?" asked Mrs Richardson.

"Like a Western," suggested Sylvie.

They washed up and swept the kitchen and went to bed.

Joanna lay and tossed and gazed at the stars through the cracks in the curtains. She saw men with guns stalking the Longmoor ponies, crouching in the bracken, aiming, firing, the ponies falling— foals, yearlings, promising three-year olds, brood mares, strong young colts, proud stallions—falling and struggling, and lying still, soaking the ground with their blood.

Carol lay three yards from Joanna and saw American servicemen, ex-cowboys, in large hats, pursuing the ponies in jeeps and on motor bikes, lassoing them, cutting their throats, dragging them back across the moors to a disused quarry where a lorry waited. She thought, it could be Ninepin, and tears ran down her cheeks.

"Are you awake," asked Joanna. "Don't cry. It won't do any good. Tomorrow we begin to act."

"It's terrible . . . Supposing they kill our ponies?" cried Carol, leaping out of bed, drawing back the curtains. Outside nothing moved. The moors looked hardly real beneath the moon; too beautiful to exist, thought Carol. The three horses were standing together in one corner of the paddock.

"They're all right," she said, pulling the curtains back into place.

"We must go to sleep; we won't be any use tomorrow if we don't," said Joanna.

Sylvie, who shared the room with them, said something in French, Carol climbed back into bed.

"The dogs will bark if anyone comes near the paddock," whispered Joanna.

"Yes," said Carol, lying down, thinking, I wish it was tomorrow already.

What shall we do tomorrow? How shall we begin? wondered Joanna. Carol started to count the sheep and presently they both slept.

Anthony lay on the put-up bed in the little sitting room, making plans. We'll search the moors tomorrow, looking for clues, he decided—tyre marks, an empty cartridge, a piece of rope—there's sure to be a clue somewhere.

Once we have a clue we can move on. He felt confident of success. When we've found who the thieves are, we can call in the police, he decided, before he too, slept.

"This looks like the farm. I'll see whether I can find Mr Hill," said Mr O'Connor, stopping the car at the end of the lane, disappearing in the direction of lights which shone softly in the dusk.

"Do you think we can get out?" asked Maggie.

"I'm sure I hear turkeys," cried Sean.

"Stay where you are. It may be the wrong place or Mr Hill may have no room for us," said Mrs O'Connor.

"What shall we do then?" asked Maggie.

"Wait and see."

Nipper was jumping up and down in the car, trying to look out of the window. Richard was sleeping huddled on his mother's lap.

Presently Mr O'Connor came back.

It's all right. We can stay in the orchard. There's

14

water and electricity quite near," he said.

They drove through a farmyard directed by Mr Hill while Nipper yapped incessantly, drowning all conversation.

The yard smelt of cow, of orchard, of apple and grass and the heather on the moors.

Mr Hill was small and solid. "Come and see us when you're ready. The wife will give us all a bite of something," he said.

The O'Connors climbed out of the car. Nipper stopped yapping. Richard started to cry.

"Well, here we are as cosy as can be; water in the yard, toilet across the way, and an invitation to supper," cried Mr O'Connor, so that they all knew he was in his cheerful mood and their spirits rose.

"And we're right next to the moors," cried Maggie.

"It looks as though there are plenty of apples on the trees. Do you think we can pick them?" asked Sean.

"I hope Mr Hill has some ponies," said Maggie.

"Plenty of time to find that out. Come on, let's get you cleaned up a bit," Mrs O'Connor told Richard.

They boiled a kettle and washed, and to Maggie the air felt softer than any air she had ever known, and though she couldn't see the moors now she could sense their nearness, and over her stole a feeling of rich content.

Sean was wondering how far it was to the sea, whether there would be rocks there, sheer cliffs or long stretches of clean white sand.

Richard's clothes were changed and his hair was brushed. Maggie dragged an unwilling comb through her fringe, pulled up her jeans and tightened her belt. Sean put a thick blue jersey over his shirt. Mrs O'Connor changed her dress.

Mr O'Connor said, "Come on, everyone. What are you all putting on your best clothes for? They know we've been travelling all day."

They walked across the orchard to the farmhouse with Nipper at their heels, and presently they were all sitting down at a large table eating bread and butter, cold beef, pickled onions, while a sponge sandwich, cheese, fruit and cream waited for them.

Gazing round the large kitchen, at the large silver cup which stood on the mantelpiece at the hunting pictures which adorned the walls, Maggie felt she had come to her dream house.

If only there are ponies, she thought, everything will be perfect.

Two sheep dogs lay under the table, their heads on their paws. Nipper had been told to wait in the porch and occasionally he whined. Outside they could hear the gentle baa of sheep.

Mrs Hill was tall and slim.

"I hope you will be comfortable here," she said, plying them with food and drink.

"Are there a lot of ponies on the moors?" asked Mrs O'Connor presently.

"Wild ones, you mean? A goodish few. But something odd's been happening to them lately. They've been disappearing," said Mr Hill.

Except for Richard, all the O'Connors stopped eating.

"It all began about a fortnight back when Jim Saunders went up on the moors to look at some of his young ones, and two of his mares were calling for their foals . . ." Mr Hill explained.

Calling for their foals, calling and calling, thought Maggie, calling and getting no answer.

"It quite upset him, and now Bill Warner finds two of

his colts seem to have vanished. Sooner or later we'll have to have a round-up and get to the bottom it, but at the moment we're harvesting, and we can't afford not to as long as the weather's fine," continued Mr Hill.

"Do you think someone's killing them? If only the foals are disappearing I suppose it could be a dog—an Alsatian," suggested Mrs O'Connor.

"It's not just the foals, repeated Maggie's mind. Someone's killing them all. For a moment her imagination flashed back to the gangs at home, and to the cafes they haunted. But it's not them, she thought, it's people who know the moors like the back of their hands, people who understand horses, people who can shoot to kill.

She ate a piece of bread and butter without tasting it, while outside the door Nipper whined again.

A mystery, thought Sean, forgetting his longing for the sea, seeing himself stalking men across the moors, headlines relating their capture by courageous young Sean O'Connor. Suddenly time seemed dangerously short. We have only a fortnight, he thought, a fortnight in which to do so much.

"Hasn't anyone an idea who it can be?" he asked.

Everyone was talking now except for Maggie; she sat still, silently listening, the food on her plate forgotten.

"It's a complete mystery," said Mr Hill.

"A real shame," remarked Mrs Hill.

"Can't the police do anything?" asked Mrs O'Connor.

And all the time the gentle baa of sheep invaded the kitchen.

"I don't know why we sit here when there's a nice fire in the sitting room. Have you had enough?" asked Mrs Hill presently.

17

They moved into a snug little room with three neat arm-chairs, two stools, a sofa, and a piano. Here Maggie managed to ask the question which had been on her mind all evening.

"Have you any ponies?" At the same time she felt the pockets of her jeans to make sure the twenty pounds were still there.

"Ponies? Plenty on the moors if someone hasn't taken them. And we've one turned out behind this house along with my hunter. You can ride then?" asked Mr Hill.

'Yes, they can both ride all right," replied Mr O'Connor, while Maggie felt inclined to add, "Not so well."

But neither she nor Sean said anything, and Mr Hill said, "I didn't think you'd be able to ride, coming from the town. But you're welcome to those two if you think you can manage them. Biddy pulls rather. Are you strong?" he asked Maggie.

"Yes, very," she said quickly.

"And the pony's all right—a bit obstinate at times like all of them. What about the little one?"

"He hasn't started yet," said Mrs O'Connor.

We can ride, thought Maggie, and saw herself galloping across the moors on a large kind hunter which pulled rather. And somehow we'll find the thieves, she decided, and bring an end to the slaughter of wild ponies.

"What's the pony called?" asked Sean.

"Jimmy; he's a little dun born and bred on the moors. He'll bring you home all right if you get lost."

"Thank you so much. It's wonderful. We love riding," said Maggie.

A little later the O'Connors walked back to their caravan escorted by a joyous Nipper. And tomorrow

18

we can ride, thought Maggie, ride and ride all day if we like, to the top of the hills and over the other side, on and on for ever until dusk comes.

"It's wonderful about Biddy and Jimmy," cried Sean, his voice shrill in the silence of the night.

"Do you think you'll manage them?" asked Mr O'Connor.

"Yes, sure," cried Sean. "Won't we, Maggie? Can't we?"

"Yes, we'll manage them," agreed Maggie, suddenly sure of nothing, happy beyond words, thinking I shouldn't be happy because of the people killing the ponies; smelling the air, the scent from the moors, the apples in the trees.

"Richard's tired out. We shouldn't have kept him up so long," said Mrs O'Connor.

"They're nice people, the Hills are," remarked her husband.

"Great," replied Mrs O'Connor.

"He said we could ride tomorrow. We'll get up early and ride all day," cried Sean.

He saw himself as a detective; he would miss nothing. Time is so short, he thought again.

"Steady on. The horses may not be fit," said Mr O'Connor.

They brought water back with them from the farmyard. They washed and pulled out their prospective beds.

"Now, no talking," said Mr O'Connor.

"I shall never sleep," cried Sean.

Mrs O'Connor kissed all her children. The light was extinguished and presently they slept.

CHAPTER THREE

Carol was up first in the Richardsons' cottage. Small and energetic, she called everyone with cups of tea and cooked breakfast. But though she didn't burn the toast, all the time her mind was already on the moors, riding Ninepin along stony paths, up and down precipitous slopes, through hock-deep bracken. She was pursuing the pony killers, saving foals from their murderous grasp; at the moment that was all she cared about, all that mattered was that the killers should be brought to justice.

Joanna awakening, thought, something's wrong, before she remembered.

"It's eight o'clock and a lovely day. The horses are still there and I've let out the dogs," said Carol, handing her sister a cup of tea.

Anthony was awake when Carol took him his tea.

"What's the day like? Are all the horses present and correct? Today is D-Day," he announced.

"Yes, they're all right. The sun's shining. Why don't you get up?" asked Carol over her shoulder as she left the room.

Soon they were all, except for Sylvie, eating breakfast in the kitchen.

"What are you doing today? I've got to get some food in," Mrs Richardson told her children.

"Riding," cried Carol.

"Looking for the killers," replied Joanna.

"What about Sylvie?" asked Mrs Richardson.

They had all forgotten Sylvie. "Can't she go shopping with you?" asked Joanna.

"She likes walking the dogs. She said so," replied Anthony.

20

Walking the dogs or shopping doesn't sound very exciting," remarked Mr Richarson.

"Someone's got to get milk and eggs from the farm," said Mrs Richardson.

"She's getting out of the washing up," pointed out Joanna, but Carol was already out of the room, grabbing a halter, running towards the paddock calling, "Ninepin, come on, Ninepin."

She felt wild and free like a pony on the moors. School and discipline seemed miles away; this is another life, this is living, she thought, slipping the halter over Ninepin's neat black-tipped ears. How can people bear to spend their whole lives in towns? she wondered, vaulting on to Ninepin from a rock.

She opened the gate without dismounting, shut it and disappeared down the path towards the farm.

In the cottage Mrs Richardson said, "I think you'd better wake up Sylvie, Joanna."

Mr Richardson found his briefcase, kissed his wife and departed. Anthony cleared the kitchen table and said, "Must we wash now?"

The three dogs, Labrador, Boxer and West Highland, lay sunning themselves outside the cottage.

In the paddock Intruder and Mulberry watched the disappearing Ninepin with pricked ears and neighed.

Waking, Maggie could see an apple tree through the little caravan window; lit up by the early morning sun, it meant the country to Maggie, two weeks in which to explore the moors. Remembering that she could ride Biddy, she clambered swiftly and silently from her bed. She found her jeans, a shirt, sweater and shoes. She dressed, plunged out of the caravan into the early morning light. Nipper, who had slept under the caravan, greeted her. The grass was wet with dew. In her ears was again the gentle baa of sheep, the soft song of half awake birds. Over everything lay a waist-high mist.

She whistled quietly to Nipper, before she hurried across the orchard, stoping for an instant to pick up a fallen apple. She climbed the gate, crossed the farmyard and entered the horses' field. Biddy was lying down watched over by Jimmy. She was a large plain brown mare, with a keen and cunning eye, and a mane which was obviously hogged at times, but now stood up straight some eight or nine inches above her neck. She sprang to her feet when she saw Maggie and trotted away across the field. She's very ordinary, thought Maggie, but 'handsome is what handsome does', she looks tireless, even if she's cunning.

Nipper had been following quietly at her heels, but now seeing Biddy and Jimmy in obvious flight across the field, he couldn't resist the temptation; in a moment he was in pursuit, yapping merrily, while Maggie stood and called in vain. Round and round they tore and every moment Maggie expected Mr Hill to appear and say that obviously she knew nothing and was never to venture near the horses again.

And now Maggie could see dozens of mushrooms scattered in tiny bits each time Biddy's and Jimmy's hoofs went over them. She rushed round the field madly picking them and all the time she was thinking, I suppose Mr Hill cultivates them, seeing him coming down to the caravan saying, "I'm afraid you'll have to leave." And it'll all be my fault, she thought, calling to Nipper again, whistling till her lips ached, saying, "Nipper, Nipper, good boy. Walkies, dinner. Come here," each time he passed nearby.

22

Soon her jersey was full of mushrooms, and there was nothing else she could take off besides her shoes, so she took them off and soon they were full of mushrooms too.

Biddy and Jimmy were trotting now, occasionally stopping altogether to kick at Nipper. He unfortunately seemed to think it was all part of the game and yapped louder than ever each time a hoof missed him by a millimetre.

Then Maggie heard a whistle and saw Sean climbing the gate. "Call Nipper. See if he'll come to you," she shouted.

He called and whistled, but both in vain.

"Whatever's happening? He'll get killed in a moment," he shouted.

"Why don't you help then? cried Maggie in exasperation.

"I'm trying to."

He ran towards her, calling, "Nipper, Nipper, come on, Nipper."

By now the little dog's tongue was hanging out, his yap had a hoarse ring and his enthusiasm seemed to be wilting.

"Come on, walkies," cried Sean. "It's awful isn't it? How were we to know he chased horses?"

"Someone will come in a moment and shout at us," said Maggie.

"Whew! You've collected some mushrooms. We'll be able to have a smashing breakfast," Sean said.

"They're not for us. The horses have trampled hundreds to pieces. The Hills will be furious, I expect," said Maggie, holding one of her bare feet and then the other above the wet grass.

"Anyway, Nipper's dead beat. He's giving up. Look, he's had enough," said Sean.

Nipper came sheepishly towards them, then changing his mind, lay down a few yards away with a guilty expression.

"Someone ought to beat him," Sean said.

"Yes, naughty dog. Bad Nipper," cried Maggie picking him up, slapping him with her hand.

"Not too hard. You're hitting him too hard," cried Sean.

Riding towards the farm, Carol heard a commotion. What can it be? she thought, and then, with a sense of panic, it's coming from the field where they keep their horses. She imagined strong men killing Mr Hill's brown hunter; she forgot that it was now nearly eight o'clock—hardly the hour for horse thieves.

She urged Ninepin into a gallop, heard the sound of yelping and thought, they're killing the sheep dogs, and felt a knot rising in her throat. Sparks flew from Ninepin's hoofs; stones rolled down the narrow path which in wet weather became a rushing stream. And Carol felt a sudden rush of excitement, because in a moment she might be face to face with the killers; she might be saving Biddy and Jimmy; saving many ponies from death in the near future. She thought, this is what soldiers must feel like in battle; I'm not afraid—not even in death.

By the time she reached the farmyard the yelping had stopped. Why isn't anyone doing anything? wondered Carol galloping into the farmyard, throwing herself off to open the gate into the horses' field.

"Honestly, I'm not hitting him hard. I've hardly hit him at all," cried Maggie releasing Nipper, who started rushing in circles, stopping occasionally to lick her toes.

24

"He made enough noise. What's that? Can you hear hoofs?" cried Sean.

"Ssh. Stop rushing around, Nipper," said Maggie. "Yes, I can—galloping hoofs. Something must be happening."

"It's the wrong time of year for hunting."

"Unless it's stag."

"But it's only one horse. Listen," cried Sean.

"I'm going to get hold of Nipper. We don't want any more trouble," said Maggie. "Come here, good dog."

"Supposing it's the pony killers," cried Sean.

"But it's daylight," objected Maggie, grabbing Nipper by the collar.

"But maybe it's one fleeing from the police. Perhaps they've been hunting him all night on the moors."

"Yes, that's quite likely," agreed Maggie, feeling excited, beginning to rush towards the farmyard dragging Nipper.

Then they both saw Carol opening the gate, waving her arms, shouting, "What do you think you're doing here? Leave Mr Hill's horses alone."

Maggie's first impulse was to flee; she hated trouble; she wanted to flee to the caravan and, if the child followed, to let her father unravel the misunderstanding. But then she recollected that her father wasn't much of a diplomat. He would become excited and say too much, making things worse rather than better.

Sean was standing apparently dumbfounded.

"We're staying in the orchard. Mr Hill said we could ride his horses," Maggie explained.

"Horse and pony," replied Carol.

"Horse and pony then," agreed Maggie, thinking, she's no older than Sean; why is it any business of hers what we're doing?

"What have you done with your shoes?" asked Carol, before she saw the mushrooms and cried, "You've been helping yourself to the Hills' mushrooms. You can't take their mushrooms."

"I'm presenting them to Mrs Hill; I've picked them for her," replied Maggie, trying to sound lofty, and wishing she was wearing shoes because she felt lowly and poor without them.

"Who are you, anyway?" asked Sean, glaring at Carol.

"I'm Carol Richardson. We have a cottage here which we come to every summer. The Hills are friends of mine. I was coming down to get milk and eggs when I heard a commotion; actually I thought it must be the people who are killing the ponies, that's why I came so fast," explained Carol with dignity, turning to look at Ninepin who was dripping with sweat.

"You know about the ponies, then?" cried Sean.

"Isn't it awful? We're determined to do something," said Maggie.

Carol looked at the O'Connors with new eyes. Until now she had assumed they were town children who knew nothing about the moors, nor about the ponies which lived there.

"You ride then? You can ride? I thought you meant to lead each other about on Jimmy when you said Mr Hill had given you permission to ride his horses," cried Carol.

"Yes, we ride. We're not expert, but we can walk, trot and canter," replied Maggie.

"Why don't you let me put those mushrooms in my pockets? Then you can have your shoes back," suggested Carol looking rather obviously at Maggie's bare feet.

"Yes, thank you, I think I will." Maggie fetched her shoes and handed the mushrooms bit by bit to Carol.

By now the sun had dried the grass, and Nipper was lying at their feet looking like a canine angel.

"They're awfully broken," said Carol.

"Have you got a brother and sister?" asked Sean.

"Yes. Anthony and Joanna."

"We passed you last night then. Our car was pulling a caravan—remember?" asked Sean triumphantly, as though he had made a great discovery.

Carol screwed up her face. She looked neat and dashing in her riding clothes.

"Yes, on the road; soon after a bridge," she said.

"I think I'm going to take the mushrooms to Mrs Hill. I came here originally to catch Biddy, but Nipper upset her and Jimmy . . ." explained Maggie.

"Couldn't you catch her then?" asked Carol. "I'll catch her for you; she knows me; they both do, because sometimes we're short of mounts and then we borrow or rather hire them."

Do they cost a lot to hire? I've only got twenty pounds and Sean has hardly anything. I'm just wondering how much we will be able to ride," said Maggie doing up the laces of her trainers.

"Can't your parents pay?" asked Carol.

"No, not really. I mean we don't like to ask. You know there's such a lot of things we need as a family, and this holiday has cost the earth."

"We've got a Vauxhall Astra, though," said Sean. "Dad works at the docks. We lived In Ireland once, but then we thought we'd like to try England and we've stayed here ever since."

"I'm taking the mushrooms now," Maggie said.

"You'd better take my coat then. I'll be warm enough without it now," replied Carol.

"Better take Nipper too. I'll stay here and help catch the horses," announced Sean.

"I seem to be taking everything," replied Maggie, before she called Nipper, and walked away across the field.

They have a cottage on the moors, she thought, that means they're rich. I expect that pony's hers. I wonder what her brother and sister are like.

"You stay where you are. They don't know you," said Carol, giving Sean Ninepin to hold.

She walked across the field thinking, they're nice and they ride. I hope the others like them. She liked doing things for people, and she knew she'd be able to catch Biddy and Jimmy without any trouble.

"Hello, Biddy. Co'up, Jimmy," she said approaching the horse and the pony, who stood watching her with pricked ears and calm eyes.

Maggie knocked at the back door of the farmhouse and waited. Round her feet speckled hens scratched busily, while further away a speckled mother was holding a piece of bread in her beak and calling to her chicks. Waiting, Maggie thought about Carol. She had never met anyone like her before; her friends at home had very little of their own besides their clothes and perhaps a bike—certainly not a pony. They talked about boys mostly and walked along the streets arm in arm giggling.

But Carol's parents are rich, thought Maggie, and she's pretty bossy too, yelling at us like that, accusing us of stealing the Hills' mushrooms. She obviously thinks she's someone.

Mrs Hill opened the door then and Maggie handed over the mushrooms, explaining what had happened and that a small girl on a pony was now catching Biddy.

"Oh, it must be Carol. I heard they were up at the cottage," said Mrs Hill. "But you keep the mushrooms, dear. We've eaten one good plateful already this year. They're early; must be the wet weather we've been having. I don't suppose you see them often, living in town."

"Are you sure? I'm sorry about Nipper chasing the horses," Maggie answered.

"Don't you worry. It won't harm them to have a bit of exercise," said Mrs Hill.

Carol caught Biddy, while Sean stood running his fingers backwards and forwards through Ninepin's mane.

"Do you want Jimmy too?" called Carol.

"Yes," shouted Sean.

"Have you a halter?"

"Afraid not."

Ninepin was quite cool now. Mum and Dad must be missing us, wondering where we've got to, thought Sean. What did she say her name was?—Carol Richardson?

Carol came towards him leading Biddy in one hand and holding Jimmy by the mane.

"Can you give me a stirrup leather please?" she asked.

For an awful moment Sean thought, what's a stirrup leather? Then he remembered.

"If I can get it off," he replied.

He was still struggling when Maggie returned.

"I've taken the mushrooms down to the caravan—breakfast's ready. And I've brought a halter for Jimmy," she said.

"Well, if you're all right now, I must go," said Carol.

"Well, thank you for everything," Maggie replied.

"If you're riding this morning, why don't you join us? We'll be leaving the cottage around half past nine. It's up there," Carol said pointing.

"Won't we be a nuisance? I mean you must be good riders and we're not—I mean we haven't ridden a lot," Maggie answered.

'But we can stick on all right," announced Sean.

"Well, that's what matters mostly, so you'll be all right," said Carol mounting, pulling up her girths automatically without fumbling, picking up her reins; looking as though she had lived her entire life on Ninepin as she cantered away across the field, calling back over her shoulder, "See you later then."

"Why did you have to say we could stick on?" asked Maggie leading the way towards the gate.

"Well, I've never fallen off and you've only come off three times. That's not much," Sean answered.

"But we've only ridden quietly. We've never galloped about on moors."

"Well, we want to catch the pony killers, don't we? That's what matters, isn't it?" demanded Sean. "If we fall off it's just too bad."

And he's right, thought Maggie, that is what matters, and as they found the stable and tied up Jimmy and Biddy in two of the stalls, she imagined men killing ponies on the moors.

"We'll be a much bigger force if we go all together. There'll be five of us," Sean said.

"Do you like Carol?" asked Maggie.

"Not much," replied Sean.

CHAPTER FOUR

"What have you been doing?" cried Joanna, as Carol reached the cottage.

"We were just going to start looking for you," said Anthony.

They were grooming Intruder and Mulberry. Tall, dressed in jodhpurs and neat shirts, they looked different from the O'Connors.

"I've been talking to the people in the caravan," explained Carol, and looking at her tidy brother and sister her heart sank a little. They won't like them, she thought, and probably the children can't ride at all, and they'll hold us up and Joanna will be furious and everyone will think I was mad to ask them at all.

"How many are there?" asked Anthony.

"Well, I only saw two," replied Carol and told them what had happened.

"They sound fun. Do you think they can really ride at all?" asked Joanna.

"Well, they said they could walk, trot and canter, and the boy said they could stick on. They were going to look for the pony killers anyway, I think," Carol answered.

"They sound okay then," Anthony said, leaving Intruder loose while he fetched his saddle.

"I hope they aren't too long coming. Did you say we would wait for them?" asked Joanna.

"No, I don't think so. I can't remember what I did say," answered Carol.

"Biddy and Jimmy haven't been ridden for some time. I hope they get up here all right."

"Don't fuss, Joanna," said Anthony. "They sound

31

fine, and the sort of people who can look after themselves."

Hardly that, thought Carol, remembering Maggie barefoot holding Nipper.

Maggie and Sean gulped their breakfast, washed up while their parents were still drinking tea.

"We're riding with the people who live in the cottage at the end of the path," explained Maggie.

"The people we passed last night on horses," added Sean.

Their father was in a gloomy mood. He had already announced that he was going to spend the morning writing poetry, and that meant he was very melancholy, and the worst of it is that it'll never be published, thought Maggie. They all hated the envelopes which came back from magazines and publishers. They were almost the only typewritten envelopes which ever came into their house, so they were easy enough to recognise.

"You'll be wanting sandwiches, then. Are you sure you've enough money to pay for the horses?" asked Mrs O'Connor.

"Can you manage them? We don't want any accidents while we're on holiday," said Mr O'Connor.

"There's plenty of cheese, and you can take a couple of eggs, if you like Maggie," said her mother.

There wasn't time to boil eggs, so Maggie simply cut some cheese and made a few rough sandwiches.

Sean reassured their father, and then they were running across the orchard in the direction of the farmyard.

"We're not late, are we?" asked Sean.

"Shouldn't think so," replied Maggie.

They hadn't watches and neither of them had

thought of asking their parents the time.

Someone had filled Biddy's and Jimmy's mangers with oats which they were now happily munching. They had been saddled and their bridles hung ready at the end of their stalls.

"I hope the oats won't make them too fresh," cried Sean; and that's just like him, thought Maggie— brave as brass till the moment comes. "We can stick on all right," he tells everyone.

"Perhaps Mr Hill will come and bridle them like the other farmer used to," Sean said.

"Well, we did in the end. Don't you remember? There's no need to panic," Maggie replied, unhooking Biddy's bridle, thinking, but then they were just ponies, not a large horse like Biddy.

Every time Maggie approached Biddy, she stuck her head out of reach; and though Maggie swung on the headcollar she couldn't pull it down by force.

Jimmy behaved no better. When Sean approached, he swung his quarters towards him in a menacing manner, and Sean retreated.

Very soon they were exasperated and Maggie was near to tears and Sean was losing his temper, when a voice asked, "You in trouble? Can't you bridle them? Here, let me do it," and a farmhand came into the stable. He was old and bent, weather-beaten, with gnarled hands.

"They do play up sometimes—artful like," he said, taking Biddy's bridle.

"She's so tall when she sticks her head up," Maggie said, looking at the old man who wasn't much bigger than herself.

"She knows you're not used to horses," the old man said, putting his thumb expertly into the mare's mouth, slipping the crown piece over her ears. "I've

33

always been with horses. There was the time when every stall in this stable had a horse in it. There you are, my gal, don't you play up no more," he said, handing the reins to Maggie.

"Are you in trouble too, son?" he asked Sean, starting to bridle Jimmy.

Presently they were all outside in the sunshine, and the old man was holding the horses' heads while the O'Connors mounted.

Sean looked appealingly at Maggie before he picked up his reins. She only reached Biddy's back after a struggle and a push from the old man. She felt very high when eventually she was in a position to adjust her stirrups and pick up the reins.

They thanked the old man several times before they rode out of the yard on two very reluctant mounts.

"Jimmy doesn't seem to want to go at all," complained Sean kicking with his heels.

"It was jolly lucky that old man came along. We'd better hurry. I'm sure we're late," Maggie cried.

"Jimmy's trying to stop," cried Sean.

"Hit him with the end of the reins then," instructed Maggie. But by this time he had stopped and it was some time before they got him going again, and all the time Maggie was thinking, they'll be gone, they won't wait, we'll be too late, and imagining the Richardsons riding away across the moors.

Eventually they started to canter along the stony track, and Sean cried, "If we are late and they've gone, we can look for the killers on our own."

Maggie was bumping up and down and feeling as if she might fall off at any moment, so she didn't reply; but at that moment she agreed with Sean; because if they couldn't control Biddy and Jimmy by themselves how would they manage them in company? We'll hold up everything if we keep falling off, she thought, and then we'll never catch the pony killers and Carol Richardson will never ask us to ride with her again.

"There's the cottage!" cried Sean, and ahead they could see an L-shaped wooden building, one storied with a veranda.

We'd better slow down, thought Maggie, but now Biddy wouldn't stop, so eventually the O'Connors halted in front of the Richardsons with a series of bounces which sent Maggie up Biddy's neck and Sean over Jimmy's ears.

The Richardsons had been standing fretting to start when they heard hoofs coming towards them. Then they had mounted.

"They're coming fast enough by the sound of it," Joanna remarked.

"I hope it's intentional," Anthony replied, "though it's bad for the horses' legs."

Carol said nothing. She wished she had never invited the O'Connors—first they were late, now they were galloping on hard rough ground, which everyone knew you should do only in dire emergency.

And then the O'Connors arrived, obviously out of control, their stirrups lost, their reins long and loose.

"Whoa, steady," shrieked Joanna, but without avail. Jimmy and Biddy stopped in a series of jerks and Sean fell off almost under Intruder's hoofs.

"Bad luck. Are you all right?" asked Anthony jumping off, while Maggie found her stirrups again, pushed her hair out of her eyes, said, "I'm so sorry. We couldn't stop. We're out of practice."

Sean cursed in Irish. "You fell very nicely," Joanna said.

"I'm all right," cried Sean, scrambling to his feet. "I'm not hurt at all."

Mrs Richardson appeared then, closely followed by Sylvie.

"Whatever's happening?" she asked.

"Nothing. Just a toss. We're just going," Anthony said.

A moment later they were all mounted and riding away from the cottage along a narrow path which wound between tall bracken, and the air smelt of peat and bog, bracken and heather, and the sky was blue. Biddy and Jimmy seemed quieter now that they were with other horses.

"I'm so glad we have you as reinforcements. We must make plans now," Anthony said.

"It's wonderful to be doing something at last! I've thought of nothing else since last night," exclaimed Joanna.

Sean took a firmer hold of Jimmy, who was tossing his head and jogging. The path wound uphill. At intervals their horses' hoofs dislodged boulders.

"I shouldn't hold him on too short a rein," advised Carol.

"I propose we simply ride over the moors today looking for clues. What does everyone else think?" asked Anthony.

"Okay," agreed Maggie, who already liked Anthony.

They began to trot and presently they reached short grass and heather.

"Let's spread out now and search for clues," suggested Joanna.

They tried to separate, but Jimmy wouldn't leave Biddy, so finally Maggie and Sean had to search together.

"What do you think of the Richardsons?" asked Maggie.

"Bit stuck up. But they can ride all right," replied Sean.

"A lot better than us," agreed Maggie, watching the Richardsons spread out across the moor, each a part of his mount. They made it look so easy, she thought. Will we ever ride like them?

"They've got ponies of their own," said Sean.

They had been riding across the heather for nearly half an hour when Biddy stopped in her tracks, threw up her head and snorted.

"What's the matter with her?" cried Sean. "Here, let me go first."

"It's all right. There's nothing there," said Maggie, trying to reassure Biddy.

"Come on, Jimmy, move," cried Sean hitting the pony with the end of his reins. But now Jimmy wouldn't move either, but clung to Biddy, who was still snorting and standing poised for retreat.

"We'd better dismount," said Maggie, jumping off. "The Richardsons will think we're pathetic," cried Sean.

"I can't help that. Biddy must be afraid of something. Perhaps she smells blood, perhaps ahead the heather's soaked in blood."

"I hadn't thought of that," exclaimed Sean dismounting, starting to run, dragging a reluctant Jimmy after him, then crying "Look, look!" There was a choke in his voice; already his eyes were smarting with tears.

"Oh no. It's so small," cried Maggie, looking at the dead foal lying alone in the heather. No wonder the horses stopped, she thought; and then suddenly she was overwhelmed with hate for the killers. How

37

could they kill it? What sort of people are they? she asked herself, gazing at the dead foal through a maze of tears.

"We'd better call the Richardsons," said Sean at last.

But they were already coming.

"What luck? What have you found?" called Joanna.

"Any clues?" shouted Anthony.

"We've found nothing at all," complained Carol.

Maggie and Sean couldn't speak; they pointed, and tried desperately to swallow the lumps in their throats.

"At first we thought you were just having difficulty with Jimmy and Biddy," said Joanna.

Why don't they answer? wondered Carol. And then the Richardsons saw the dead foal.

"Oh, no! Is it quite dead?" cried Carol, leaping off, leaving Ninepin loose, running to the foal's head, bending down.

"We'd better find out how long it's been dead," said Anthony.

"Poor little thing," said Joanna.

Having lived all their lives in the country they were used to death. Their dogs had died, their first pony, their favourite bantam. So the sight of the small foal slaughtered so early in life didn't shatter them as much as it did the O'Connors, who still stood without speaking.

Anthony examined it, while Joanna held the horses and looked on; only Carol shed tears into the heather.

"It's so sweet and it had a little star," she said. "They must have killed its mother; otherwise she would still be here. Oh, how I hate them!"

She couldn't stop crying. She thought, he might

have been a wonderful jumper, a hunter, a prize moorland pony—a champion. Or he might have roamed the moors with his herd, wild and proud and free. She tried to stop crying because the O'Connors were there and then she saw that Maggie's lashes were wet, and her own tears fell faster than ever in the heather.

"He's been dead some time," said Anthony, cool and efficient. "But how he was killed I don't know. We'd better take him down to the farm and see whom he belongs to."

Before, searching for the pony killers looked like fun, something to amuse us during the holidays, thought Joanna, but now it's deadly earnest. Now we'll search day and night if necessary.

"Will that help? Shouldn't we go on searching?" asked Maggie.

"You mean the scent's still warm?" asked Anthony.

"I wish we had guns—lots of them," cried Sean.

"Hear, hear," cried Carol.

"Don't be silly Sean. How shall we get him down anyway? The horses won't go near him," Maggie said.

"Carry him. We'd better split into two parties; one to go down, one to continue the search for clues. What do you think, everyone?" asked Anthony.

"That sounds the best idea," answered Joanna. "But how shall we decide who goes?"

"It'll have to be two big people who go down because of carrying," said Maggie, and she prayed that she wouldn't be chosen, because she hated the thought of carrying the foal, because more than anything she wanted to mount and ride on and on across the sunlit moors, which seemed too peaceful for sorrow, to ride on in search of the killers and in an effort to forget the foal.

"The three of us had better toss. Odd man stays to search," said Anthony finding three coins, keeping one and giving the others to Joanna and Maggie.

They tossed, caught the coins, clapped them on the backs of their hands. "Heads," cried Anthony.

"Tails," said Joanna.

Everyone looked at Maggie. Either way I go, she thought and said, "Heads."

"I'll carry him most," said Anthony, looking at her woe-begone face. "I expect I can manage him all the way. I can stop and rest if I get tired."

"I'll do my share. I'm quite strong really," said Maggie.

Anthony handed her Intruder. "I'll do the first shift anyway," he said. "I don't suppose you like the thought of it much. You're not used to dead animals like we are. We've seen plenty—dead stags, foxes, our own chickens, dogs, kittens . . ." He picked up the foal and, putting it across his shoulder, began their journey back.

"See you later, Maggie," Sean said.

She took a horse in each hand and followed Anthony.

"I'm glad I haven't got to go," said Carol.

"So am I," cried Sean.

"We're the lucky ones," Joanna said.

They mounted their horses, which had stood suspiciously all this time. They spread out again across the moors and rode on and on towards the sun.

CHAPTER FIVE

Afterwards Maggie never liked to remember that journey back. It was gloomy and endless and as they grew tired, the foal seemed to grow heavier. The horses lagged, jibbed at every suspicious clump of gorse, every tree stump, nervy and afraid.

Because of this, whoever led the horses was always a long way behind the foal carrier, and although Anthony remained reasonably cheerful, Maggie became steadily more gloomy.

At first they tried to talk, but neither could hear what each other said, until finally it seemed easier to walk in silence.

Maggie's thoughts remained centred round the dead foal—how had it died? Where was its mother? Why had it died? Whatever she did, her mind came back to that.

Anthony made plans. Tonight we'll search the moors, he decided, it's lucky our horses are fit. We'll post ourselves as spies, and see whether the killers return to collect the foal. In a sense he was elated by their find because at least it meant progress, a beginning, a clue of some sort.

When they reached the Richardsons' cottage, Anthony said, "Let's stop here to revive." The dogs greeted them: "Solomon, Julius and Morag," said Anthony.

They dumped the foal outside the gate, tied up their horses. "Are you thirsty? I am," said Anthony.

Maggie's legs were stiff and her back ached because she wasn't used to walking or riding so far. The sun had disappeared but it was stiflingly hot. The dead foal haunted her and she knew it would

41

continue to for many days and nights.

Mrs Richardson greeted them. "You're earlier than I expected. Where are the others?" she asked.

"I'll explain in a moment. Can we have something to drink please? This is Maggie O'Connor, Mum," said Anthony.

They sat and drank cider and Anthony related the events of the morning, while outside the sky darkened ominously and a breeze blew round the cottage in threatening gusts.

Sylvie came in while they were still talking and smiled at Maggie. "It will rain soon, will it not?" she asked.

At last Anthony said, "Well, I'd better go, Mum," and they went out into the threatening afternoon, and Anthony said, "You ride the last bit. You look all in. I'm madly energetic at school and I'm pretty fit." So Maggie gratefully mounted Biddy, Anthony gave her Intruder and they continued down the hill.

Now that Biddy could see the farm she hurried, while Intruder, reluctant to leave the cottage, dragged.

The first rumble of thunder sounded as they reached the farm; the sky was very dark now and the moors looked wild and angry, cruel, gloomy and remote.

"I hope the others get back all right," Maggie shouted to Anthony as they entered the farmyard.

"They should be all right. Joanna knows the moors like the back of her hand," Anthony replied.

But Sean doesn't, supposing he gets separated? Lost? Falls off? wondered Maggie, and she was filled with dreadful foreboding. Anything can happen, she thought. Why did I leave him? Mum and Dad will be horribly surprised when I arrive alone. And now nothing seemed beautiful any more, not the moors, not the orchard, not even their caravan which she could see now among the apple trees. With a sudden wave of homesickness Maggie longed for her usual surroundings, for the safety of the streets, for her giggling girl friends as company rather than the determined boy who strode resolutely forward, a dead foal across his shoulder.

Anthony, turning to smile at Maggie before he knocked on the farmhouse door. His arms and shoulders ached, he felt muzzy from drinking two glasses of cider on an empty stomach; but most of all he felt triumphant, because they had ridden over the moors to find a clue and they had found it.

Jimmy didn't want to continue across the heather alone; every few moments he stopped and tried to turn back, but Sean, determined not to be defeated in front of Joanna and Carol, forced him on with voice and legs and the end of the reins. At first the three of them rode with little more than ten yards between each horse, shouting remarks to one other.

"I wonder how the others are getting on," shouted Carol.

"How do you like being at the farm, Sean?" shouted Joanna.

"It's smashing," answered Sean.

"Jimmy's awfully nappy, isn't he?" asked Carol.

What's nappy? wondered Sean, but not wishing to display his ignorance, he called back, "Yes, sometimes," and gathered that he had given the right answer.

They drifted farther apart until they couldn't hear each others' remarks and stopped talking.

And now that Jimmy realised Sean was in earnest,

43

he walked eagerly with a quick short stride, avoiding holes and stray boulders, seeming to enjoy the expedition. Because Jimmy was going well he felt as though he had spent his life on a horse. He remembered instructions he had read in a book on riding last summer, and adjusted his leg position, moved his elbows closer to his sides and shifted his weight farther forward in the saddle. He felt wonderfully free, miles from anywhere on the wild and lonely moors. In front he could see hills, and beyond them lie the sea, he thought. He was sorry for children at his school who spent the whole summer playing in sunless back gardens and noisy streets. He imagined relating his own adventures to them when term began again. He noticed that the sky was growing darker, the moors more gloomy, but it seemed to suit his mood; even the threatening ominous breeze which stirred the heather and the short rough grass only seemed part of the scene; none of it warned him, as it should have done, of the storm approaching.

Now nearly a quarter of a mile away Carol recognised the first signs; she knew at once what was coming. She could see Joanna and she turned Ninepin towards her. We'll just have time to find a shelter, she thought; waving and shouting.

"There's a storm coming." She pushed Ninepin into a gallop forgetting the existence of Sean.

Joanna had been wondering how Maggie and Anthony were faring, when she heard Carol shout, and noticed the darkening sky. We'll just have time to reach the gully, she thought.

"We'll have to gallop," she called, closing her legs against Mulberry's sides, thinking, I hope Anthony and Maggie have reached the farm by now.

The gully had been a refuge from storm, from

welcome relations, from angry parents as far back as Carol could remember. It was really simply a dip in the ground sheltered on all sides by trees, a perfect hide-out and a place kept secret by the Richardsons from friends and foes alike.

Carol and Joanna reached the gully as the first drops of rain fell. They charged through the trees and once inside the horses stopped automatically, swinging their quarters towards the storm.

"We've made it," said Carol.

"But where's Sean? Wasn't he with you?" cried Joanna, preparing to ride back into the face of the storm.

"Look!" cried Carol. "Look! They've been here." She couldn't believe her eyes; there was a shiver down her spine and an empty feeling in her tummy.

Joanna turned back and now she too could see the heap of rope, the charred embers of a fire, an empty tin of tobacco.

"It needn't be them," she said. "It could be picnickers."

"But the rope . . ." cried Carol.

Yes, the rope, thought Joanna, and now hideous visions leaped to both their eyes and they stood in horrified silence while the storm burst with lightning and thunder across the moors.

"What shall we do?" asked Carol at last.

"Come back here tonight. I've got the shakes. Have you?" asked Joanna.

"Yes. They come here at night but why? I shall never like the gully again. It'll always make me remember the foal."

"We'd better look for Sean next. He can't be far away," said Joanna, turning Mulberry's head towards the storm again.

"Why didn't he follow us? Won't he have found shelter?" asked Carol.

"We can't just leave him to his own devices. He doesn't know the moors like we do."

"Shouldn't we take some evidence with us if we're leaving?" said Carol.

"Not if we want them to come back. We mustn't arouse their suspicions."

"What about our hoof-marks?"

"With any luck, they'll think wild ponies have been here."

"Oh, isn't everything terrible? Why does Sean have to be so stupid?" cried Carol.

Their horses were reluctant to leave the gully; once outside it, they could see nothing but rain, and there was another flash of lightning followed immediately by a tremendous crash of thunder, which seemed to echo backwards and forwards across the moors.

"It's hopeless. We'd better go back," said Joanna.

"He must have found some sort of shelter by now," replied Carol.

"I don't know where. There isn't any other shelter, besides here, for nearly a mile."

Hardly any rain fell in the gully, and when the next crash of thunder came it was muffled by the trees. But now neither Joanna nor Carol felt at home in their favourite hiding-place; it was as though it was haunted by the presence of the pony killers; it didn't belong to the Richardsons any more. The rope and the tin had turned the gully overnight into an enemy camp.

"I think the storm's going to go on for hours," said Joanna, wondering what everyone would say if they returned without Sean, whether a search party would be sent out to look for him, whether the O'Connor parents would be frantic with anxiety.

Joanna sat silently astride Mulberry, imagining Sean meeting with a variety of fatal or nearly fatal accidents. Already she had become resigned to catastrophe; first there had been the horror of the dead foal, then the storm blotting out everything—there had to be the third thing. And that third thing obviously concerned Sean. If she had been younger she would have cried with despair; as it was she sat, silent sunk in the deepest gloom.

Mr Hill opened the door of the farmhouse.

"Hello, Anthony. What a day to be out. Come in; don't stand there getting wet," he said.

"Look what we've brought you. We found the poor little beggar lying dead in the heather," Anthony answered, and there was a lump in his throat as he spoke. He pointed at the foal.

Maggie was dripping wet now, the rain ran from her hair down her neck; her jeans clung to her legs, her shirt to her back. She stood thinking the same thing over and over again: I hope Sean's all right. I hope they're looking after Sean. Supposing he doesn't come back? At this moment she hated the moors and she didn't listen to Mr Hill and Anthony, but turned to look at them again and saw only the outlines of the sloping hills blanketed in rain. And somewhere they're up there either still riding or sheltering under a tree, she thought.

"Poor little devil. Looks a bit like poison to me. I'd better get on to Jack Dawson at once," said Mr Hill.

"What about the police?" asked Anthony.

"Best find out how he died first. We'd look silly if it's natural causes," replied Mr Hill.

At the word poison Maggie turned. She saw now that Mr Hill was in his socks. He looked as though he had been sitting in front of a fire reading the paper. "Who's Jack Dawson?" she asked.

"The vet. Sounds the best idea. We're going up there tonight," Anthony told Mr Hill, indicating the moors by a jerk of his head.

"You'd better be careful. What does your Dad think about the business? Does he mind you gallivanting about the moors looking for these criminals?" asked Mr Hill.

"Hasn't said much about it yet," replied Anthony.

"Well, you be careful. I don't like the sound of them. Now you put your horses in the stable and come in and get warm. The young lady behind you looks wet to the skin. I'll just slip down to the telephone box and call Jack Dawson." Mr Hill retreated indoors obviously in search of his boots.

There was another flash of lightning and more thunder as Anthony and Maggie crossed the farmyard together.

"I hope Sean's all right. He hasn't ridden much," Maggie said.

"Oh, he'll be all right with Joanna and Carol; they're used to picking up people. We'd better run or we'll get wetter still, if that's possible," replied Anthony.

They tied up and watered their horses, and then spent some time drying them with handfuls of straw.

"This must be a change from living in a town, isn't it?" asked Anthony.

"Yes. But once we lived in Ireland and we spent last summer on a farm, so it isn't completely new," explained Maggie.

"Whatever do you do when you're at home? I don't

know what we'd do if we hadn't the animals," said Anthony.

Maggie thought, what do I do? before she said, "Take Nipper for walks, watch people playing tennis on the courts."

"I should think Biddy and Intruder will be all right now. Let's see whether Mr Hill has returned yet," suggested Anthony.

The yard was a pool of water. Rain was pouring from overflowing gutters as well as from the sky. And now the buildings were lit by a long sheet of jagged lightning.

"We'd better run like mad," cried Anthony.

Mrs Hill flung the door open as they reached the house. It was warm in the farm kitchen. A sleepy fat black cat lay on a chair in front of the Aga. A kettle hissed and bubbled, saucepans simmered.

"Mr Hill is still at the telephone box. I've made you some tea." said Mrs Hill.

It was a very safe domestic scene after the raging storm and bleak angry moors outside. It made the past few hours seem more like a dream than reality.

"You got down here just in time," said Mrs Hill, handing them both cups of tea.

"The others are still up there," answered Anthony. "But they'll be all right; if they've got any sense they'll be in the gully and that's nearly rain-proof."

"It's no day to be out in, gully or no gully. What about this girl's brother, is he up there too?"

Maggie had been lulled by the warm atmosphere, now anxiety came back.

"Yes he is," she cried. "Do you think he'll be all right?"

"He's with Joanna and Carol," Anthony explained.

"Oh, then he'll be all right, I expect. Jimmy's a

good pony and will bring him home if he gets parted from the others. There's no sense in worrying." But the reassuring note in Mrs Hill's voice had the opposite effect on Maggie to what was intended. She thought, they're anxious too.

"Now stop worrying. There's no point in it. I think I hear my husband," said Mrs Hill.

Mr Hill came into the room. "I managed to get him, or rather his wife did on his radio. He's coming along straightaway," he said.

CHAPTER SIX

The crash of thunder took Sean by surprise. He looked round expecting to see Carol and Joanna but suddenly the moors seemed empty, as though every living thing had sought shelter except himself. For a second he was seized by a kind of animal panic; then as the rain fell, he thought, it's only a thunderstorm, Carol and Joanna can't be far off. I'll find them in a moment. Jimmy was calm but refused to advance into the face of the storm; in a matter of seconds they were both soaked to the skin. Sean hit Jimmy with the end of the reins, kicked him with his heels, shouted, but all in vain; the dun pony wouldn't go forward so the only choice was to go back. Sean turned him round and said, "Go home then."

Joanna and Carol will guess I've gone home, he thought. The rain was falling in solid sheets; it was almost impossible to see anything. The saddle and bridle were running with grease and water. Jimmy advanced in jumps, his tail tucked between his legs, his head bent. But Sean was determined to enjoy

himself. This is an adventure, he thought, not everyone has the excitement of being lost on moors in a
thunderstorm. After a time, however, he started to
feel more anxious. Jimmy seemed as lost as himself.
He began to imagine he had seen the boulders they
passed at least twice before. Supposing we're going
in a circle, round and round the same piece of ground?
he thought, with a funny feeling in the pit of his
stomach. Odd figures seemed to rise up from behind
boulders, making Sean jump and feel weak with
fright until he saw that they were only dark faced
sheep. He started to call, "Carol, Joanna, Joanna,
Carol. Where are you?" But not for long because it
seemed hopeless to compete against the falling rain,
and the constant crashes of thunder heralded by the
longest and brightest flashes of lightning he had
ever seen. He felt very lonely now. The moors seemed
endless, and all his confidence in Jimmy had gone.
He thought, is this really happening to me? and it
seemed incredible.

He was afraid now and shouted, "Get a move on
Jimmy. Why don't you take me home?" and kicked
the dun pony in the ribs. Will they look for me? he
wondered. Joanna was supposed to look after me—
why didn't she? He felt furious with everyone. Then
suddenly Jimmy shied and Sean rolled off sideways
into a damp bed of heather.

He tried to grasp the reins, but Jimmy swung on
his hocks, jumped Sean and disappeared into the
storm at a steady trot.

"It's clearing now. Look, it isn't really raining any
more," exclaimed Joanna.

"Hurray. Now we can carry the news to the farm,"
cried Carol.

51

"You mean about what we've found? But first we must search for Sean," replied Joanna.

They rode out of the gully. The sky was striped grey and blue; the moors smelt wet and peaty; drenched branches swept their legs, sent rain cascading down their necks, before they were right in the open, searching miles of moors hopefully with their eyes.

"Not a sign," said Joanna at last.

"No. Where can he have gone?"

"Home with any luck."

They didn't need to express their feelings to one another; each knew the other was racked with anxiety. With one accord they turned their horses' heads towards the farm.

"These holidays seem doomed," announced Joanna. "Everything seemed such fun at first; now it's just terrible."

Ninepin and Mulberry were glad to be going home; they had been cold in the gully; now they hurried over the rough ground with pricked ears.

"Things must look up soon," said Joanna.

"What about the bogs?" asked Carol.

"You mean for Sean? I hadn't thought of that," replied Joanna. "But Jimmy won't go into one; he's got too much sense," she added a moment later.

The ride back seemed endless to Carol. They rode as fast as they could; the sun came out and the sky turned blue; they passed a herd of ponies grazing peacefully, over them a buzzard flew searching for prey. Quite soon it was difficult to believe there had been a storm at all; only the lovely smell of earth after rain remained. It became a day for success, for picnics, for family expeditions, for horse shows and gymkhanas, thought Carol, remembering that today the East Pathlock Show was being held, and wishing that she was competing with Ninepin instead of riding in search of Sean across the moors.

At intervals Joanna and Carol called "Sean, Sean, where are you?" but without much hope and without success.

At last they came to the cottage, and, leaving their mounts loose, ran inside.

"Have you seen Sean O'Connor?" they called.

"What's the matter? What's happened?" cried Mrs Richardson running towards them, while the dogs began to bark.

"There hasn't been an accident," cried Joanna, catching a glimpse of her mother's face.

"We've lost Sean," said Carol, and now she was home she felt like bursting into tears.

"Lost Sean? But where? Not on the moors?" asked their mother.

"Yes, on the moors. We lost him in the storm. We hoped that by this time Jimmy would have taken him home. Are you sure he hasn't gone past here?" Joanna asked.

"I can't be sure. I might not have heard him. After all, Jimmy is only a little pony; his hoofs don't make much noise," said Mrs Richardson.

"The dogs would have heard him though. They always bark if a horse goes by," cried Carol.

"What an awful day this is—first there's the foal, then this new catastrophe."

"Yes and that awful storm. If there hadn't been a storm . . ." said Carol.

"We wouldn't have found those things in the gully, though," replied Joanna.

"Sylvie's gone down to the farm. She was bored stiff following me around. I think you two had better go

53

down too; you can tell Mr Hill about his pony then and perhaps he'll let the O'Connors know about Sean. Then if he doesn't turn up soon someone will have to organise a search party," said Mrs Richardson. "You really are a couple of asses losing Sean."

The horses had gone round to the stable. Ninepin had opened a sack with his teeth and was busily devouring oats; Mulberry had installed himself in a loose-box.

"Will you be all right? Or would you rather I came down and did the explaining?" asked Mrs Richardson.

"We'll be all right," replied Joanna mounting.

Jack Dawson said, "I think I'd better take him home for a post mortem. Whose is he?"

"Not one of mine. I couldn't really say; he's too young to have been branded. I say he isn't mine, but then again he might be. There's no knowing," replied Mr Hill.

They were standing together outside the farm-house. The chickens had reappeared. Because of the rain the farmyard smell was stronger than before.

"It's a shame whoever he belongs to," said Jack Dawson, bundling the dead foal into the back of his van. "It's time this monkey business stopped; why don't the police do something?"

"I expect they will all in good time," said Mr Hill.

"Have you informed them yet?"

"No. I didn't want to until I knew how the foal had died. Look silly if it was natural causes."

"Okay. I'll ring them when I know," said Jack Dawson and he drove furiously away.

It must be annoying to spend your life trying to save things and then come across some people killing simply for the fun of it," said Anthony.

54

"If that's all it is," said Mrs Hill.

All this time Maggie had been silent; she had stood trying not to look at the foal while small nimble Jack Dawson prodded and poked, exclaimed in anger, bundled it into the van and drove away. But now the moment had come—she had to leave the others, go down to the caravan and tell her parents about Sean.

"Well, what do you think about it all, Miss?" asked Mr Hill turning towards her, while she stood wondering whether to give an explanation or simply to vanish.

"About the foal you mean? Awful. . ."

"She's worried about her brother. He should be all right though; he's with Carol and Joanna," explained Mrs Hill.

"My parents will be worried. I must go and tell them," Maggie said.

"Wait a moment. Here comes Sylvie," said Anthony. They all thought that she must have come with news of some sort.

"Hello. What's happening?" called Anthony.

"What news? Should there be news? I haven't seen the bad men. I've seen no men," she cried, gesticulating. "It was so dull. I came down to see life, to see what happens," she explained.

"Nobody has turned up at the cottage yet then?" asked Anthony.

"I see no-one," repeated Sylvie.

"You had better come in and get changed; or else go down to the caravan," Mrs Hill told Maggie.

"Don't worry, he'll turn up all right. If he doesn't, then we'll all turn out and look for him. He's in good company if he's with Joanna and Carol. They know the moors as well as any of us," said Mr Hill.

"I'll go down to the caravan," replied Maggie. Everything had begun to seem rather unreal; too much had happened already; life was assuming the proportions of a nightmare; if only Sean would come riding into the yard, thought Maggie, and then they all heard hoofs quite clearly coming down the path towards the farm.

"That sounds hopeful," said Anthony.

If only it's Sean, thought Maggie.

"But it's probably a false alarm," continued Anthony.

"Let's hope not," said Mrs Hill.

They all hurried towards the farmyard gate. The moors looked fantastically beautiful now lit up by the afternoon sun. 'The vacant wine-red moors', thought Maggie remembering a poem by Stevenson. I shall always remember this moment, she decided, a moment of suspense, and she was certain that Sean was one of the people riding towards the farm, so certain that she started to call, "Sean, Sean," to open the gate and run out on to the path, to stand and stare and see only Joanna and Carol riding to meet her.

"He's not here," called Joanna in her well-bred voice which Maggie suddenly hated. Hasn't he arrived? We were hoping Jimmy would have brought him home."

"We searched and searched . . ." said Carol.

Maggie stood quite silent. So he is lost, she thought and glanced at the moors, and wondered what they were like at night, whether there were bogs and hidden pits.

"I'm surprised at Jimmy," exclaimed Mrs Hill.

"We lost him in the storm. I can't explain how it happened because I don't really know," Joanna told them.

"We tore to the gully, we thought he was following," added Carol.

"We'd better go back and go on looking," Joanna said, pushing a damp lock of fair hair under her skull-cap.

"I shouldn't go straight back. He may turn up yet. Stop here a little while," said Mr Hill.

"Here come Mum and Dad," cried Maggie, and they all turned to see Mr and Mrs O'Connor picking their way across the wet farmyard.

"We were wondering where you were, my girl," said Mrs O'Connor. "You look wet through."

"Sean's lost," cried Maggie and she was glad that it was said, at last.

"It's our fault. We were supposed to look after him," Joanna confessed.

"More likely his—little monkey," said Mrs O'Connor in the tones of deepest affection. "Always up to something, that's Sean."

"You mean up on the moors?" asked Mr O'Connor. It wasn't necessary for Maggie to talk; everyone seemed to be explaining at once.

"He should be all right on Jimmy," said Mrs Hill.

"We searched for ages," cried Carol.

"I don't know how it happened . . ."

"It was the storm; that's what did it. . ."

"If he doesn't turn up in a moment we'll organise a search party."

"Yes, there are bogs, but Jimmy should keep clear of those."

Voices were so agitated or excited that Nipper got a wrong impression and thought an outing was about to take place and tore round in circles yapping shrilly.

"I'd better slip back to the caravan. Richard's all

alone. He was asleep when I left," said Mrs O'Connor presently.

"Better take Nipper. Stop it, stop it, I say," cried Mr O'Connor.

"And you come along too. We can't leave you getting pneumonia," Mrs O'Connor told Maggie.

They called Nipper, set off across the orchard towards the caravan. The morning seemed to have happened a long time ago to Maggie; she remembered her feeling as she climbed out of bed; how full of promise the day had seemed. Why does everything have to go wrong now? she thought. Mr Hill will most likely never let us have Biddy and Jimmy again now.

"Do you think he's all right? How did you get parted? We can't have anything happen to Sean, us on holiday and all," said Mrs O'Connor.

"We drew lots. I was to come down, he was to go on looking," explained Maggie. Her heart felt as heavy as lead. She knew her mother was near to tears. The clock on the little shelf above the cooker told her that it was a quarter past three. Its steady relentless ticking maddened her. Richard sat up in bed and started to cry. Maggie remembered that she hadn't eaten since breakfast; but the thought of food revolted her. She put on another pair of jeans and a sweatshirt. Why did we have to come, she thought? Supposing Sean disappears in a bog? Supposing he is killed by the pony killers or is never found? Nipper had jumped on her bed, covering it with muddy paw marks. She wanted to cry with exasperation, despair and bad temper. Her mother was dressing Richard. There seemed no room in the caravan at all.

"Where shall I hang these?" asked Maggie, holding up her wet jeans and shirt.

"Listen, listen, I think I hear a pony coming along the path," cried her mother.

In a flash Maggie was out of the caravan. Her hopes rose to dizzy heights; perhaps after all everything was going to be all right. It must be Sean. She streaked across the orchard, climbed the gate, crossed the farmyard. Everyone was still there, or had they left and come back? They stood in a little group surrounding Jimmy. And when Maggie saw them she broke into a walk; for the moment her mind refused to grasp the fact that Jimmy had returned without Sean, even though she had dreaded the possibility from the moment she had started walking and riding down to the farm with Anthony and the dead foal. Her father was running his hands through his hair; Mr Hill appeared to be reassuring everybody, Carol was crying. It seemed fantastic to Maggie that she already knew all these people, that in so short a time they had become part of her life.

What will Mum say, she thought?

She saw that Jimmy had no stirrups on his saddle, and that his reins were broken. Nipper, sensing some sort of catastrophe began to yap again. A chicken announced to the world the arrival of an egg. Biddy neighed to Jimmy.

"Hello, Maggie," called Anthony. "Do you see what's happened? Jimmy, but no Sean."

"Yes, I see," replied Maggie, and there was a knot in her throat which kept rising, and made her voice croaky, and she thought again, why did we have to come?

CHAPTER SEVEN

Sean tested his eyes first and found that he could still see; he next explored his teeth with his tongue and found that they were all intact. His legs obeyed his commands with their usual alacrity and in a matter of seconds he was on his feet surveying his position.

Jimmy was disappearing at a steady purposeful trot. Sean called, "Jimmy," without much hope. On all sides of him the moors stretched wild and uninhabited except for the black-faced sheep and presumably wild ponies. He stood thinking, at least I'm having an adventure, but the thought failed to cheer him. He felt horribly alone, completely lost and the first tentacles of fear were already reaching for his brain.

He looked in all directions; there seemed no reason for walking in any one—East, West, South, North. The shining sun didn't cheer him, because he could sense that it was already afternoon. He hadn't a great many hours left before dark, though plenty to get him home if only he knew the way.

He felt very helpless as he stood there trying to make up his mind what to do next. The endless miles of grass and heather frightened him. If only there was a house somewhere in sight, or even a road, he thought, feeling very small and insignificant amid so much space.

At last he started to walk steadily in what he hoped was a southerly direction and as straight as possible. He picked out a distant boulder and directed his footsteps towards it, when he reached it he chose another one. He remembered someone telling pace that they could keep up all day, hour after hour. He tried to slow his own footsteps, but fear of darkness made him hurry, though because it was August there was still many an hour left before dark.

He wasn't used to walking over rough ground and soon he had a blister on one heel and then the other. He was stiff from his hours in the saddle. And several times he longed to sit down and rest if only for a few minutes, but the thought of the moors at night drove him on. He stopped once to eat the food he had in his pocket, the sandwiches made by Maggie in the morning, the biscuits his mother had pressed on them; and all the time the thought hung over him, supposing Maggie sends a search party and all the time I'm walking away from it? It was a thought which terrified him, which made food stick in his throat, which made his walking seem useless. But he continued all the same, because he had to do something, he couldn't simply sit and hope for deliverance. He could sense the hours passing as he walked; constantly he wondered what they were doing at the farm. Had Carol and Joanna turned up there? Or were they still searching for him? What was Maggie doing? Had Jimmy arrived?

A little later he began to imagine headlines in the morning papers, 'Boy lost on moors'. 'Pony returns without rider'. 'A search party has been organised to comb the moors for Sean O'Connor missing since Friday' ... His photograph would be on the front page, probably the toothy one his father had taken last year at the seaside. His friends at home would read the news, say, Whew, look what's happened to Sean. Thinking of that made him feel better. After all not everyone gets in the papers, he thought. He then began to think about Jimmy. Supposing he doesn't return? Supposing the killers get him? The thought made him run until he realised the uselessness of it. The ground was more peaty now, there were less and less boulders but more and more sheep. Perhaps there'll be a shepherd; they must look at the sheep sometimes, he thought, and he started to call, "Hello there, hello," the sound of his own voice so small and useless in so much space made him panic suddenly. He was seized with fear and started to call, "Mum, Mum, help," and to run blindly stumbling over the sodden ground, while tears streamed down his cheeks. He felt only blind with fear as he ran, but after a time he stopped through sheer exhaustion. He stood and stared across the moors, and saw in the distance the faint outline of hills which had been with him all day. He seemed to have made no progress at all. If the ground had been dry, he would have given himself up to a fit of despair. As it was he stood and thought, I shall die here. What's the use of going on? I shall never reach anywhere.

He sat down at last and the dampness in the ground seeped through his trousers and unobtrusively dusk stole over the moors.

Orders went out for a search party. Mr Hill decided to ride Biddy, so there was no mount for Maggie.

The Richardsons fed, watered and rested their horses. Sylvie volunteered to return to the cottage and break the news to Mrs Richardson. There was an air of urgency now at the farm; the dead foal was forgotten, though Mr Hill visited the telephone box again and could have easily telephoned Jack Dawson. The O'Connors stood about useless and stricken. Mrs Hill provided everyone with tea and biscuits and gave them substantial sandwiches for their pockets.

The collies were called to assist in the search; a sense of urgency grew. Richard stood by his mother weeping; even Nipper seemed sobered at last.

Presently two farmers rode into the yard on stout cobs. Weather-beaten men arrived on foot, dressed for the moors, followed by a variety of dogs.

Carol was told she could not go.

"You're too young," said Mr Hill, who had emerged as a leader of men.

"But I know where we last saw him," cried Carol, with tears smarting behind her eyes. It'll be awful to be left behind, to lie in bed without sleeping, she thought, supposing he's in a bog, and it's all our fault.

"Joanna is going to take us there. I tell you, you're too small by half," said Mr Hill.

"That's right enough," agreed one of the mounted farmers.

Maggie stood by her mother thinking, is this really happening? It seemed so like a description in the paper, a description one read with sympathy for the people involved but without ever thinking, it might happen to us.

Joanna stood aloof from the others. She was afraid. Supposing I can't lead them to the place? Supposing we don't find him? Whatever happens it'll always be my fault, because I'm older than Carol, so it was my duty to look after him, she thought again and again. She felt racked with worry. Each moment of waiting unnerved her a little more.

Anthony was thinking about the killers. Supposing they're up there tonight. I hope they don't get wind of this expedition, he thought. Optimistic by nature, he couldn't visualise anything serious happening to Sean. He was more concerned with the pony killers. Not for a moment had he forgotten the foal carried to the farm so laboriously. If he had, his aching arms and shoulders were there to remind him.

More people kept arriving. However many people did Mr Hill telephone, or did the news travel by word of mouth, Maggie wondered?

Mr O'Connor was to join the foot contingent. He had found himself a stick, and was taking Nipper. He towered above most of the other men; his mouth was set in a grim line, his expression was resolute. He didn't look the sort of man who would be crossed by anyone.

Mrs O'Connor's face was tear-stained but now she was calm. "You stop with your mother," Mr O'Connor had told Maggie and reluctantly she had agreed.

Presently the Richardsons fetched their horses and mounted. Mulberry looked tired already. She was run up and covered with dry sweat. Mr Hill mounted Biddy. The sun had gone. Evening had come while they waited, a dull evening which promised an early night for August.

The Richardsons pulled up their girths. "You're to leave us at the cottage, Carol. If we don't find him soon we'll call up a helicopter," Anthony told her.

Goodbyes were said. The search party filed out on to the moors, Joanna leading.

"Good luck," called the people left behind and someone shouted, "Good hunting."

The yard was very quiet now. "I suppose we might as well go to the caravan," said Mrs O'Connor.

Maggie's "Yes," came out as a whisper.

"Come inside. Richard can play in the little sitting room," said Mrs Hill.

Maggie and her mother followed Mrs Hill inside

like sheep. Maggie had no energy left for anything. She could only think, I wish I was up there searching with everyone else; it's much worse to be here waiting, wondering, hoping.

"I expect he'll be all right. You mustn't fret," said Mrs Hill.

"I can't help feeling he might have hurt himself, seeing him up there with a broken leg or something," confessed Mrs O'Connor.

Maggie was given the job of amusing Richard. Mrs Hill made more tea.

"I can't remember anyone ever getting hurt on the moors, not badly I mean, except an old shepherd who died up there—that was heart failure, and Sean's not likely to get that at his age," said Mrs Hill. "You want to remember it's summer too. He won't die of exposure this time of the year."

"Then there's the people who kill the ponies. Who are they, do you think?" asked Mrs O'Connor.

"I wish I knew, but I doubt that they'd go hunting a little boy," answered Mrs Hill.

"Goodbye. See you later, Carol," said Joanna.

"Keep your ears open and your eyes skinned," advised Anthony. "Anything may happen tonight."

"Goodbye. Best of luck," said Carol, turning towards the cottage, feeling a little sick at heart, while her mind still travelled with the riders up and up to the top of the moors.

"Hello. What news? What's the latest?" cried Mrs Richardson coming to the door followed by Sylvie and the dogs.

"No, nothing," replied Carol, who was suddenly tired beyond words. "He's probably dead in a bog by now."

"Don't be so gloomy. Turn out Ninepin and then come and have some supper. "I'm just getting it," said Mrs Richardson, undoing the chestnut pony's throat lash, running up the stirrups.

"The soup, it boils over," cried Sylvie rushing indoors.

Everything is normal—soup for supper, Mum helping me turn out Ninepin, the cottage looking just the same as usual, thought Carol. But if Sean dies, nothing will be like it was ever again. He'll haunt me for ever.

"The sooner you're in bed the better, darling," said Mrs Richardson leaning across Ninepin to kiss Carol. "I wish the others were home. I don't know what Dad will say when he comes in."

"But some of us had to go. After all he was with us. If I hadn't invited the O'Connors to ride with us, this would never have happened," cried Carol, appalled by the thought.

"You're determined to blame yourself, but the O'Connors didn't have to ride with you, they did because they wanted to, and there was no mention of you looking after them, was there?" asked Mrs Richardson.

"No, not really, but I meant to all the same." Together they turned out Ninepin. It was really dusk now, and the moors were kinder, their few sharp edges softened by the drowsy light.

Presently Mr Richardson arrived home.

"Well, what's happening? There are all sorts of rumours circulating," he asked.

His wife explained, while Carol drank orange juice, because she didn't feel like anything else, and Sylvie hovered wanting to join in the conversation but unable to find the right words fast enough.

"Well, I'm going up there too," cried Mr Richardson, when he had heard of the day's events.

"But you must have something to eat, it's all ready," cried his wife.

But he wouldn't wait. He called the dogs, collected a walking stick. "We've got to find the boy. And while I'm up there I might as well have a look for the killers," he said.

"I wish you'd eat something first. Do be careful," said Mrs Richardson.

The cottage seemed very empty when he had gone. "It's like the war. Or ten green bottles," said Mrs Richardson.

"I wish he hadn't taken the dogs," replied Carol.

"I'm not afraid," said Sylvie.

But although they ignored the fact, the cottage was suddenly full of ghosts, of creaking doors and suspicious shadows.

They ate their supper mostly in thoughtful silence, Carol's mind riding with Anthony and Joanna, feeling the swing of their horses' strides, the mixture of excitement and fear while her ears heard the sound of hoofs and her nose smelt the wet moors.

"It's a good bit farther yet," said Joanna. It's getting so dark, she thought. Shall I be able to find the place where we last saw him? Supposing I can't?

"I know where the gully is anyway," said Anthony suddenly beside her. "Is Mulberry tired? Intruder feels all in. I suppose the truth is he's out of condition for the moors."

"Yes, she's terribly tired. She feels as though she's done a whole day's hunting, but I suspect some of it's put on, because she didn't want to turn out again," replied Joanna.

"They've had rather a rough deal really. It's not as though they can know it's a matter of life and death," said Anthony. He was still certain that soon they would find Sean, roaming lost but unharmed across the moors. He was still more interested in a search for the pony killers, and it was for them his eyes combed the dusk, looking behind each boulder, inside clumps of bracken, behind and round the occasional bush they passed.

Never did I dream I would lead an expedition like this, thought Joanna. Poor Sean, where is he now, she wondered? She wished that Mulberry had more energy and that it was dawn instead of dusk so that they would have more time. They proceeded at a steady relentless trot; unfit hunters sweated and puffed, but their riders had no mercy—this is a matter of gravity, they thought, and drove their tired horses on.

"We're nearly there now, aren't we? This is where Maggie and I left you, isn't it?" Anthony asked his sister.

"Yes, yes, I think so," replied Joanna, suddenly not certain of anything.

"We're nearly there," Anthony called to the horsemen behind.

Some riders let their horses walk. If you turned round you could see the torches of the searchers on foot. Looking back, Joanna thought, somewhere among them is Sean's father, and she imagined him tall and anxious, towering above the rest of the party searching for his son. It's really a nightmare, she thought. Why don't I wake up and find it never happened. And riding into the gathering darkness she prayed, "God let us find Sean O'Connor."

They came to the spot where Carol had fled to the

gully. The moors seemed silent now except for their breathing, for the champing bits, for the creaking of leather. It was uncannily still, and far above a pale transparent moon appeared, but as yet there seemed no stars.

"It's unearthly up here tonight," said Joanna with a shudder.

"Is this where you last saw him?" asked Mr Hill.

"Near enough."

"What did you say his name was?" someone asked. And when Joanna had replied, they all began to call: "Sean! Hey son, where are you?"

"Young Sean O'Connor, we're looking for you."

And far away the hills between them and the sea brought their cries back again, silly, futile, unanswered, so that to Joanna it seemed that the hills were mocking them, that the moors said, "We keep our secrets."

Anthony sat biting his nails. Why did they have to call? We'll stumble on Sean soon and they're simply giving the game away to the pony killers. He saw no more hope of surprising the men, and sitting slumped on tired Intruder, he thought, why did Carol have to ask the O'Connors to ride with us? and why later did she and Joanna have to lose Sean?

"Might as well go on," said someone.

"It's a bad business," announced Mr Hill.

A sense of seriousness had grown in the expedition while it stood; until now everyone had expected to find Sean quite easily. Now there was the mention of bogs, of fast flowing rivers, and more than once the pony killers.

"Better spread out," said Mr Hill.

Except for the faint light from the moon it was dark, and it was growing colder. The horses without exception wanted to turn back. Joanna thought, I've brought them to the spot, that at least is something.

A man at the back called, "I've lost a shoe."

"Well, you won't find a blacksmith up here, mate," replied an unshaven farmer riding a pony.

They began to spread out. It's all horribly like this morning, thought Joanna. Let's hope we all know our way home. Some of them began to call again, "Sean, Sean, Sean . . . Where are you?."

The only woman in the expedition joined Joanna. She was tall, with the longest legs Joanna had ever seen.

"You're a Richardson, aren't you? You were with him this morning. You must be feeling terrible about it," she said.

"Yes, yes I am, it's like a nightmare," Joanna replied and with a sense of annoyance felt tears of self pity rushing to her eyes. "It's all so horrible. I don't know why it had to happen. Poor Sean and it's really all my fault," she said. She felt like crying on someone's shoulders—anyone's. Or else hiding herself away to weep alone. But she held back her tears. "It was all because of the pony killers," she said.

Anthony rode beside Mr Hill. The day seemed suddenly the longest of his life, longer than hunts which started with mucking out at five and ended with rugging and bandaging at seven, longer than whole days spent at horse shows followed by a journey home. And there's still the whole night left, and if necessary we'll continue the search tomorrow, he thought. If only we could accomplish everything at once—find Sean safe and sound, capture the killers, he thought.

"I'm sorry for Mr and Mrs O'Connor. It's not as though they're country people either," said Mr Hill, and Anthony wondered what difference that was supposed to make.

"They took it very well—didn't panic or anything," continued Mr Hill.

"I just hope he isn't in a bog. He can't come to much harm otherwise," said Anthony.

Farther back the expedition on foot advanced slowly, searching methodically, beating each bush, beating even the heather and the bracken with their sticks.

Mr O'Connor spoke to no-one and so unapproachable did he appear that no-one spoke to him.

CHAPTER EIGHT

For a time Sean must have dozed for he seemed to be running along lamplit streets pursued by bloodhounds while Maggie stood waving to him from a roof top. When he returned to reality he thought for a moment. Where am I? and for a terrifying second he didn't know.

He stood up and found that he was wet from the dew which had fallen and from the damp ground. He looked at the sky and saw the moon appearing, and thought, I must find my way home, and then, they must have sent a search party by now. Mum and Dad wouldn't let me be lost up here and do nothing. After that he began to reproach himself; he had been silly losing sight of Carol, and why, oh why, did he have to fall off Jimmy?

And then he remembered the pony killers, and thought, perhaps after all this is my lucky day, perhaps I shall capture them and again he saw headlines and this time they read: 'Boy catches pony killers'. 'Mystery solved by young boy'. There'll be no more killing then, he thought, finding that he could stand upright and walking on with fresh purpose in his stride.

Presently he remembered that there might be bogs, and began to test each piece of ground before he put his full weight on it. Once he saw a herd of ponies grazing close together, their tails swept the ground and there were several foals, who industriously grazed beside their mothers with bent knees because their legs were so long.

Some time later his immediate surroundings began to change; there were more boulders, streams and rivulets dancing in the moonlight, clumps of trees. More than once he thought he could smell the sea, an unwelcome smell now which terrified him, and told him all too clearly that he had been walking in the wrong direction. The caravan seemed miles and miles away. He thought, supposing I go on roaming like this for days and days until I die of starvation? He started to shake with fear, and he was cold, colder than he had ever been before, although it was summer. When he saw another herd of ponies he called to them, hoping that the sound of his voice would dispel his own fears. They raised their heads and watched him. Dun, roan, brown and chestnut they looked beautiful in the moonlight, and their beauty seemed to warm him a little and help him to forget for a moment his own plight. And then suddenly their heads turned in another direction. They stood quivering with pricked ears and Sean thought, the pony killers, and was shaking with fear again. For a second he was powerless to move, and then, when his legs would obey his demands again, the worse moment was past and he was thinking, supposing I can catch them, seeing himself in the headlines again.

But before he had time to plan anything a head appeared above a boulder and he was face to face with a man of medium height, wiry, with stony, grey remorseless eyes.

There was a short silence, which Sean felt shouldn't last. He was relieved to see that there was only one man and he had no gun. He said "Hello," using the tone of voice of one of his school friends at home.

"We'd best be going to the caravan now. Thanks for all your hospitality," Mrs O'Connor said.

"That's all right. Are you sure you wouldn't like to put the little boy to bed here?" asked Mrs Hill.

"No, we'll be going," replied Mrs O'Connor.

"Come on, Richard," said Maggie.

"Sean, Sean, Sean?" cried Richard who adored his brother.

The caravan was untidy and unwelcoming when they reached it. Neither Maggie nor her mother had the heart to tidy it. Mrs O'Connor seemed suddenly to have aged ten years. She moved like an old woman and instead of chattering as she usually did, she said almost nothing at all.

Maggie had bitten her nails to the quick. She put Richard to bed, and because all the time she was imagining the search party on the moors, she forgot to give him a last drink of milk. Presently he began to cry and after that it was ages before he slept. When at last he was silent Maggie saw that there was a moon and a million stars.

She stood outside the caravan looking at the sky until her mother said, "I wish we could do something."

And at that moment Maggie remembered Jimmy.

"Do you mind if I go? Everyone's gone in the same direction, that's the silly part of it. I could go the opposite way," she cried. "I could take Jimmy."

And Mrs O'Connor, who had no imagination, so couldn't imagine Maggie getting lost too, said, "Yes, if it'll do any good," and took a handkerchief from her pocket and wiped her eyes.

Maggie kissed her mother. Already, because she was glad to do something, she felt better. I'll find him, she thought; and I've got longer legs than Sean, so I'll manage Jimmy all right.

"Goodbye," she cried, running away across the orchard before Mrs O'Connor could change her mind.

Jimmy was standing forgotten and neglected in the stable. Caked with dried sweat and wet earth, tired and dejected, he looked a sorry sight, but Maggie had no time for pity. She found his tack and she supposed because it was a matter of life and death and on such occasions one is often given extra strength, she managed to bridle him without trouble.

She didn't think of asking anyone whether she could take Jimmy, she simply mounted and rode through the open farmyard gate, pushing Jimmy with her legs when he tried to stop.

It was exhilarating to be riding by moonlight. It was something Maggie had never done before. If she hadn't been searching for her brother, she could have enjoyed it, as it was she rode desperately, tortured by her imagination. Luckily Jimmy was sure-footed and when she tried to ride him directly into a bog, he jibbed and after urging him forward for several minutes, it dawned on her that the ground might not be safe and she turned him round.

She lost all sense of time and nothing seemed real any more. Once she thought, I'm riding better, I keep forgetting I'm on a horse, perhaps I look like the Richardsons now, part of Jimmy as though I had ridden all my life. She was sorry now that she had left her mother. She could imagine her moving about the caravan anxious and alone, unable to turn on the radio for fear of waking Richard. And all the time Jimmy was trotting, his neat roan ears pricked, his hoofs picking their way carefully over the rough ground; though he had been far in the morning, he seemed tireless now. Why on earth did Sean fall off, Maggie wondered? Jimmy's easy to ride. He's a dear pony, and she leaned forward to kiss his neck, before she began to worry about Sean again.

"I can't think where he can have vanished to," said Joanna's companion. "Poor little chap."

The moors had never looked so empty to Joanna. Except for the search party they seemed totally devoid of man or beast. Was it always like this at night? she wondered, because never before had she crossed the moors by moonlight.

Mulberry felt on her last legs. There is nothing more tiring than riding a tired horse. Any moment Joanna expected Mulberry to stumble, lose her balance and fall. She sat stiffly waiting for catastrophe and because of this her back and legs started to ache. And all the time her companion continued talking, "It's good of Mr Hill to organise a search party. It's not as though he isn't a very busy man," she said and, "Poor child, you must be worried," which annoyed Joanna, who didn't consider herself a child.

It wasn't long before the rest of the expedition were only distant horsemen, indistinguishable by the light of the moon. And Joanna began to feel sleepy; every few moments she would doze, see Sean in some ghastly situation and return to reality with a jerk.

It was after one of these dozes that she heard her companion say, "My dear, I think your mare's lame. She's limping."

Joanna straightened herself with an effort. The news seemed too much to bear. She let her body go with the swing of Mulberry's walk and felt the limp in the mare's stride. Her companion had halted and was already dismounting. I shall have to go back alone, thought Joanna. She felt afraid as she dismounted, and remembered laughing in the past at people who had been afraid. She had been brought up to scorn fear, to mount the horse no-one else dared to ride, to cross deserted fields alone in the dark, to fall off horses and remount without a qualm.

"It may be a stone in her hoof. I've got a collapsible hoof pick in my pocket," her companion said.

But already Joanna knew it wasn't that, but a sprain or a strain, something which would render Mulberry lame for months and months. There was nothing to see at the moment. Mulberry's rather long cannon-bone was clean on her near fore, but her off fore was hot, particularly down by the fetlock. This was the leg that she had sprained two years ago when the Richardsons, in a fit of over-enthusiasm, had hunted her four times in a fortnight. And Joanna remembered that tendons once strained are never quite the same again.

"Perhaps she'll be all right in a moment," said her companion.

"No, it's a strain or a sprain, something serious. It probably started as a strain and I didn't notice and

76

now it's become a sprain," said Joanna hopelessly. Standing there holding her dejected, exhausted mount, she thought, I'm fated. I shall have to go back now, walk back leading Mulberry. She started to turn round, thinking it's miles and miles, feeling quite unable to speak, weighed down by the chain of disaster which had pursued her throughout the day.

"I'd better come with you," said her companion.

"No, please don't. I'm all right. I know the way," said Joanna, suddenly overwhelmed by a longing for solitude. "But we can't have you lost, too."

"I know the way. I think you should go on searching. It's Sean O'Connor who matters," replied Joanna, already walking away leading her limping mount.

Her companion didn't follow and presently she was completely alone on the moors, except for Mulberry, who walked painfully behind her.

Mum will be fed up; she hates having a lame horse, thought Joanna. Mulberry will probably never be the same again. She felt resigned to disaster now. She remembered her father saying, "It's courage which gets you through life. The courage to get up again when you've been knocked down." She thought, I must have courage, and the soft thud of Mulberry's hoofs on the grass and heather seemed to echo the word to say, "Courage, courage, courage."

Farther away the rest of the search party moved forward resolutely. Some people were still optimistic, " We'll find him soon. He's probably asleep in some bracken, poor little fellow," they said. Others shook their heads. "He may have hurt himself when he fell. There are plenty of bogs a little further on," they said.

Anthony shut his mind against the catastrophe. He was still treating the expedition as an adventure,

He refused to foresee disaster. He said presently, "I think I'll walk for a bit—give Intruder's back a rest," and slid to the ground. He found he was stiff; for a moment he could hardly walk.

"Bit early to start that, isn't it?" asked Mr Hill.

"He was out most of the morning," replied Anthony, stopping to pat Intruder's bay neck.

"So was Biddy if it comes to that," said Mr Hill.

"Well, it'll do me good to stretch my legs," replied Anthony. He loosened Intruder's girths.

"Well, mind you don't stumble into a bog. I don't want to have to pull you out," said Mr Hill, stopping to light a pipe, his second since they had left the farm nearly three hours ago.

Fifty yards away two or three people had dismounted and while one held the horses the others walked backwards and forwards through a clump of bracken, beating at it with their feet and riding sticks.

"You'd think they were looking for a fox instead of a boy," said Mr Hill.

"What we need are tracker police dogs," replied Anthony.

"We'll have the police out tomorrow if we haven't found him, and a helicopter," promised Mr Hill.

"If that happens I should think the killers will disappear for ever," Anthony said.

"And a good thing, too."

They continued in silence, and Anthony thought suddenly of Maggie. What's she doing now? Sitting in the caravan? Waiting? Hoping? he wondered. He was desperately sorry for her and for Mrs O'Connor. It's awful to stay at home, to have nothing to do but wait, he thought. He had liked Maggie when they had gone down to the farm together. She had carried the foal without complaining; she was sporting for a town girl and she didn't talk all the time like Joanna's girl friends.

"How long are the O'Connors staying?" he asked Mr Hill.

"Was to have been a fortnight. But I suppose it all depends now. I couldn't say," he replied.

"This must be awful for them. But we must find him soon," said Anthony.

Mr O'Connor was still alone; it wasn't intentional but from the moment he left the farm he forgot the other searchers. If they spoke to him he didn't hear them. To them he was foreign, and formidable; gradually they had drifted away from him until he walked by himself, tall and aloof. Now, if he was tired he didn't notice it, nor did he feel his shoes rubbing his heels. Occasionally he would stop and stand staring in all direction, and once he called, "Sean. Where are you, lad? Sean!"

For him there was poetry in the night; in spite of the fear and sadness in his heart, he couldn't help admiring the wild landscape, the distant hills and the strange light they held beneath the moon.

He had a watch and it was nearly midnight when a voice called, "Hi, there. Are we both on the same quest?" The man waving to him was followed by three dogs.

"I'm looking for my son," replied Mr O'Connor and walked on, his eyes searching the heather, the bracken, the grass and behind boulders for Sean.

The man behind caught up with him. "I'm Richardson," he said. They shook hands.

"I feel I'm to blame and I do apologise. He was with Joanna and Carol, wasn't he?"

"That's right enough. But they're not to blame. He should have stuck on the pony," replied Mr O'Connor.

Ahead of them they could see a wild herd of ponies. A buzzard wheeled suddenly in the sky.

"I hate to see one of them—it always makes me think something's dead somewhere," exclaimed Mr Richardson pointing at the bird. "I brought the dogs, but they don't seem to have picked up anything yet. I suppose you'll be informing the police if we don't find him tonight," said Mr Richardson.

"Yes, I'll be seeing them in the morning," agreed Mr O'Connor.

They walked on together, Mr Richardson talking, Mr O'Connor giving brief replies.

CHAPTER NINE

The ponies had fled. He looks strange and rather frightened, thought Sean, eyeing the man he had discovered.

"What are you doing up here? These moors are no place for a boy of your age at night."

He speaks well, thought Sean. He wasn't afraid now, only pleased to have his terrifying solitude ended. But I should be afraid, he thought.

"I'm lost. What are you doing if it comes to that?" asked Sean.

"That's none of your business."

"Why do you carry rope round your waist?" asked Sean, feeling bolder.

"You ask too many questions," replied the man. "Someone should teach you to mind your own business and to keep your mouth shut."

"Sorry, sir," Sean said. "But can you tell me the way to Mr Hill's farm? I should like to go back there. And what's your name?"

"You can call me Charlie. Are people looking for you? I'm on the run—see. So you'll be in trouble if you open your mouth and talk," Charlie said, and suddenly Sean was sorry for him. Then he remembered the foal. If this man could kill foals he was capable of anything. Sean hardened his heart. "I'll think about it. I may have to tell them," he replied.

"Look, I've got plenty of food, and I'll tell you your way home, but only if you'll keep your mouth shut—see," said Charlie. "We can have a little secret together."

I don't want a little secret, thought Sean, longing suddenly for his name in headlines, imagining himself returning to the farm with a complete description of the killer.

"I've got sausages, plenty, and bread enough for two," said Charlie. And now Sean discovered he was ravenous. At the mention of sausages his mouth began to water, and he could see the bread, crisp and new, spread with butter.

He looked again at Charlie, and saw that he was very sunburnt, with a jagged scar above his left eye, and that his hair needed cutting. His shabby flannel trousers were too big for him and were held up by a belt drawn tight round his small waist.

"Well, what do you say? Sausage, bread, a nice cup of tea to wash it down?"

Sean stood wavering, a victim to conflicting emotions. His sympathy was with Charlie, until he thought about the foal; then he hated him. His mouth watered for the sausages, and at the mention of tea he had become unbearably thirsty. Then he remembered the Richardsons and how they had all set out in the morning to find the killers. But we didn't imagine there would be only one and that he would look like Charlie, he thought, and the day seemed impossibly long, because the morning seemed to belong to years ago.

Charlie watched him wavering. "All cooked over a little fire," he said.

Sean conjured the fire, a thin line of smoke climbing through the trees. The search party, if there was one, would be sure to see it. He could imagine the sausages spitting in a pan. It so happened that his favourite dish at home was sausages and baked beans. They'll see it, so in a sense I shall have led them to the killers, he told himself, they'll see the smoke and know at once.

"All right," he said.

"That's better, and remember it's our little secret. I don't like to think of you wandering up here alone, but I have to think of myself," Charlie said. "Now, come along with me, and don't forget tomorrow morning none of this ever happened."

Charlie walked very fast; Sean had to run to keep alongside. His shoes were black and very worn. They looked out of place on the moors. Come to think of it, he looks like someone on the run thought Sean, and he hasn't shaved today either. I'll have plenty to tell them at school, he thought, before remembering that he was bound to secrecy.

"What's your name?" Charlie asked.

"Sean."

"Irish?"

"Dad is," Sean replied.

He thought he could see the first rays of dawn gleaming over the hills. Where are we going? he wondered. Supposing something terrible is going to happen? He looked at Charlie again, suddenly panic-stricken. But in spite of his appearance there was some goodness in Charlie which communicated itself to Sean, who remembered his father saying, "There is honour among thieves," which meant, Sean supposed now, that the worst people can be honest.

"Where are we going, Charlie?" he asked again.

"Wait and see."

"You did say sausages, didn't you, Charlie?" he cried.

Dawn had come and still Jimmy wasn't tired. It was a type of dawn Maggie had never seen before. In spite of her anxiety it made her feel quite happy for a moment when the first light of day lit up the hills. Gradually the sun seemed to lay a yellow carpet for her, stretching from the highest peak to Jimmy's hoofs, which still moved neatly, without effort, like clockwork, Maggie thought.

It was the sort of dawn which brings hope to failing hearts, and it gave Maggie new courage. She started to call again, which was something she hadn't done for hours. She stood in her stirrups and called, "Sean, Sean." She passed a herd of deer which watched her warily. There must have been fifteen or more and there was one magnificent stag.

After that she kept stopping, standing in her stir-rups to search the landscape better, and she resumed calling for Sean at intervals.

Later she decided to walk, and dismounting, found she was stiff. She wasn't tired, which surprised her because it was another day and she hadn't slept.

And then presently she thought she smelt the sea, and now at last she had reached the hills. Knowing

Sean's love of the sea she was sure he had gone over the hills, and she started to run. She was very hot now, and she judged the time to be between five and six. If only I find him by the sea, if only he isn't drowned, she thought. There was a straight wide path up the hills wide enough for a car, but rough and unkempt—all right for a jeep or Land Rover though, thought Maggie, suddenly imagining ponies being loaded into a boat, or rather dead foals. They probably take them to Belgium or France, she thought, puffing now, thinking they'd load them early in the morning if the tide's right or if there's a suitable place and then, supposing they've got Sean, supposing they're taking him too, just to keep his mouth shut. Her throat felt dry, tears rushed to her eyes, which she brushed away with her hand. I may be in time, and if I'm not, I may find some evidence, she thought. Jimmy was lagging, suddenly tired of the whole expedition. He was hungry and thirsty; he was nearing a part of the moor he didn't know, where the grass was wiry and grew on sand. He could feel the ground changing under his hoofs. He didn't want to go on. Maggie was merciless. She hit him with the reins and her hands when he stopped, screamed, "Come on, will you. We must go on. Move." He followed reluctantly, dragging at her arm, and now they could hear the rise and fall of the sea, see gulls in the sky and smell seaweed.

They had nearly reached the summit of the hills. Another August morning had begun. We'll be too late, thought Maggie. Why didn't I ride faster? If only I had known the sea was here. A dozen more stumbling steps and Maggie stood gazing down at the sea, at rocks and sand in a bay, at wheeling gulls, and at a boat moving slowly away from the shore.

There seemed no point in going on. My intuition was right then, Maggie thought, something is going on around here, because that doesn't look like a fishing boat. It was a perfect bay for nefarious deeds, shaped like a horseshow, with plenty of rocks jutting far out into the sea.

She stood and stared at the boat. There seemed to be only two men on board; but if they've got Sean he's probably down below, thought Maggie.

The path she had climbed led down to the bay. She looked for hoof-marks on it but the surface was rough and gave no clues of any other people or ponies passing that way recently.

"We'd best go back as quickly as we can," Maggie told Jimmy, while around them the gulls started to cry mournfully, and far, far away a train hooted.

"I wish we could find the lad," Mr Hill said. "I wasn't worried at first but now I am."

"We seem to have been searching for hours. My watch says four thirty. Is that right?" asked Anthony.

Biddy looked tired, quite unlike the mare Maggie had mounted in the yard nineteen hours ago. Mr Hill was no lightweight, and he rode in the old-fashioned way, sitting on the back of his saddle.

"Yes, four thirty," he agreed, and Anthony thought, that's when one's resistance is at its lowest.

"He must have kept going all the time, and in the wrong direction, too," continued Mr Hill.

"He had a fair start on us," replied Anthony, who was still walking, mechanically now.

Presently there was a shout from two distant riders and Anthony's hopes rose at once. He mounted and followed Mr Hill who was already cantering away, hitting Biddy on the side of her neck with his whip, as he sat straight and upright in his saddle.

Anthony stood in his stirrups urging Intruder with his legs and the horse, seeming to realise there was something important at stake, galloped courageously over the rough ground. But they were to be disappointed.

"We've found a handkerchief. Could it be his?" asked Mr Cobbett, a tall farmer, as though Anthony was expected to know all Sean's hankies by heart.

Anthony dismounted and looked at Intruder's tucked-in flanks, before he examined the handkerchief, which was small—a child's he guessed—with little Scottie dogs on it. In the circumstances it looked strangely pathetic. The surroundings were too wild and unkind for such a little handkerchief.

"It could be his. It's a child's anyway," said Anthony before he noticed Miss Sims, Joanna's companion, standing alongside Mrs Yule, a well-liked local landowner.

He couldn't take his eyes off Miss Sims for a moment. His first thought was, where's Joanna? Why aren't they together? There must have been an accident. Or did they simply drift apart? He saw Joanna in a bog, riding alone all through the night, mixed up with the killers.

He had met Miss Sims once before at the blacksmiths and so he knew her name, that she lived with her ageing mother, and that she arranged the flowers at the church. He couldn't believe such a person would purposely desert his sister.

The farmers were still discussing the hankie. It had made them sentimental. "Poor kid, poor little fellow," Mr Cobbett said.

"Such a nice little chap, too," remarked Mr Hill, just as though Sean was already dead.

Anthony rode across to Miss Sims. "What's happened to my sister, Joanna? You were together." Unintentionally his voice was accusing.

Miss Sims looked taken aback. She stood for a moment staring at Anthony in surprise and bewilderment, before she said, "Oh, you're Anthony, her brother. I'm so sorry, I didn't recognise you at first. She had to go back; her mare's lame. I wanted to accompany her but she insisted that she would rather go alone, she said that I was more needed in the search for the little boy—so unselfish."

Anthony saw Joanna riding alone, or worse still probably walking. For a moment he was too angry to speak; he could only think, why was Miss Sims so silly? Why didn't she stay with Joanna regardless? Then he thought how furious his father would be if he knew, and started to wonder why he himself had been so stupid, why he had left Joanna to ride with Miss Sims, when he searched with Mr Hill, who was probably the most reliable member of the expedition.

"She seemed so sensible, I'm sure she won't come to any harm," said Miss Sims.

But Anthony stood silent, every moment seeing worse catastrophes in his imagination.

CHAPTER TEN

Down at the farm another day had started; the cows were in their stalls waiting to be milked; Mrs Hill was cooking breakfast for herself. In the caravan Mrs O'Connor dressed Richard with a heavy heart. If it hadn't been for her youngest child she would have been searching the moors by now; as it was she hadn't slept and her eyes seemed to have gone farther into her head and were surrounded by red rims with dark shadows underneath.

She had always distrusted the country, now she hated it. The apple trees outside, the clear sky, the warming sun, held no joy for here. Give me a street with people and noise any day, she thought, and if we'd stayed at home this would never have happened. After she had dressed Richard and put the kettle on, Mrs Hill appeared. "Come and have breakfast. You don't want to stay down here alone," and because she was a warm-hearted woman she put her arm round Mrs O'Connor and added, "He'll turn up all right. Don't you worry."

They called Richard who was talking sadly to himself about Sean, and the three of them went across the orchard together towards the farmhouse.

Carol wakened. She was still sitting up and every bone ached. She thought, what happened? Then she remembered and sprang from bed with one swift leap. She rushed to the window. Ninepin was looking over the gate. The sun was already high in the sky. She could hear her mother in the kitchen. Sylvie was still asleep.

She couldn't believe that the night had passed without anything happening. But the dogs were not visible and Intruder and Mulberry had not returned. Life resembled a nightmare again as she went downstairs without hope, feeling washed out, useless, and a hundred times more guilty.

She called, "Mum," as she entered the kitchen, and, "Mum, has anything happened?"

Her mother was making toast. She looked exactly the same as usual, which surprised Carol. Outside

Ninepin walked up and down the paddock fence like a caged tiger at the zoo.

She could see now that it was a wonderful morning, and somehow that seemed to make everything much worse.

"No, nothing, not a thing," replied Mrs Richardson, and listening to her voice Carol knew she was anxious, and that seemed to kill her last remnants of hope.

"What do you think's happened? Do you think he's dead? He can't be dead. He mustn't be dead," cried Carol. So strong for a moment were her feelings of anxiety, remorse, guilt and fear that she felt she'd go mad standing there in the familiar little kitchen.

Her mother put her arm round her. "I think he's probably been walking in the wrong direction. Most likely he's found by now and soon Dad, Anthony and Joanna will return. Anyway, it's useless to get in a frenzy about it," she said.

"Can I go and look?" cried Carol, longing for action.

"I think there's plenty of people looking. I'll tell you what—you can go down to the farm after you've eaten some breakfast and find out if they've heard anything," said her mother.

They had breakfast together in the kitchen, and presently Sylvie came down and inquired after Sean. When told there was no news, she cried, "Still lost? But that is terrible. And Mr Richardson, does he still search? and Anthony and Joanna?"

"As far as we know. We really know nothing," replied Mrs Richardson.

"Poor little boy," cried Sylvie.

"Can I go now?" asked Carol, already on her feet. A moment later she was bridling Ninepin, thinking how long ago yesterday morning seemed, how awful it would be to know in advance exactly what the future held for you.

Ninepin was anxious to start. He pushed his nose into the bridle and seized the snaffle bit. He was off the moment Carol put her foot in the stirrup. He seemed excited by his night alone; he tore down the path to the farm.

Mrs Hill was shaking a mat outside the back door. Breakfast was over; Richard chased a chicken round the yard. Mrs O'Connor sat knitting in the kitchen, dry-eyed, slumped in the most comfortable chair.

Carol knew at once that nothing had happened. If Mrs Hill's grim set mouth hadn't told her, the appearance of Mrs O'Connor would have told her that there was no news, that as far as they knew Sean was still lost on the moor.

Drearily Carol dismounted, but by now the two women had seen her and their faces were filled suddenly with hope.

"Have they found him? Oh, they've found him." they cried. They ran towards Carol, their tiredness forgotten, smiling, waving excited hands. And to Carol, standing suddenly still, it was the worst moment of her life.

"No, there's no news," she said, and burst into tears.

Mulberry would go no farther. Joanna unbuckled her bit from her bridle, tied her to a small tree by her reins attached to the noseband. She then picked grass until there was a little heap in front of Mulberry. Earlier she had watered her at a stream. She kissed Mulberry now, twice on her neck, once on her shoulder. She said, "I'll come back as soon as I can."

She stood and looked at her mare, who nibbled the grass, resting her injured foreleg.

"Well, goodbye," said Joanna, before she turned and started in the direction of home alone.

She was very tired. She had to consciously order her legs to walk, to keep saying, "One, two, one, two," and to herself, "Courage, Joanna, courage."

It was quite warm now and in the occasional trees she passed, birds were singing. The weather reminded Joanna of happier occasions, which became far happier in her memory than they had been at the time. Once she thought she saw some people on foot in the distance. If she had run she might have caught them up; but she had no energy left and only called, "Hello," and "Help," and "Anyone about." The distant figures didn't even turn their heads, and it made Joanna feel small and insignificant to find her voice so useless amid so much space. She felt like an ant as she continued down the well-known path, like something which would never alter anything, nor matter very much.

"Joanna," Mrs Richardson cried, "What has happened? Where have you been? What's happened to Mulberry? Have you seen your father?"

"Dad? Is he lost too?" replied Joanna.

"No, searching like everyone else. Have they found Sean?" asked Mrs Richardson.

Joanna tried to explain what had happened, but because she was exhausted nothing seemed coherent any more, and she muddled the sequence of the events, couldn't remember whom Anthony was riding with, couldn't describe anything and kept saying Mulberry when she meant Sean.

Finally she sank into a chair and said, "Oh, Mum I'm so tired." Now that she was home she only wanted to sleep and sleep. It would have been easy for her to shut her eyes then and forget everything, but she remembered Mulberry with a rush of pain and remorse.

"She's tied to a bush, all alone. She looked so sad when I left her," Joanna murmured.

"Who?"

"Mulberry." At that moment her mare mattered more than anything. She forgot Sean and remembered only Mulberry's pained eyes when she hit her.

"I wish you had come before. Carol's down at the farm; she could have consulted Mrs Hill. They have a trailer and might know of someone with a jeep or Land Rover who could help."

"We must do something," Joanna said. But her brain wouldn't work any more; it would only show her Mulberry limping painfully, tied to a tree resting her aching tendon, Mulberry who had carried her so often gallantly and without faltering to the end of a hunt, who was to Joanna the sweetest horse in the whole world. Joanna sat, her tired shoulders sagging, and the sun streamed into the kitchen showing up the dust under the table.

She didn't speak, because her words had ceased to make sense. She couldn't understand what her mother said, because she couldn't concentrate any more.

At last Mrs Richardson said, "Come on, old thing, wake up. Bed's the only place for you."

She led Joanna protesting to the girls' bedroom, while Joanna said over and over again, "But what about Mulberry? We can't leave Mulberry there."

Her mother helped her undress, pushed her into bed, tucked her up.

"Now you go to sleep and when you wake up everything will be all right," she said.

Joanna's head sank into the pillow. She didn't see her mother leave the room because she was already asleep.

It was a long walk to the gully and Sean was very tired. He wanted to call, "Wait, wait," to Charlie like he had to his mother when he was seven. He would trail miles behind her when she took him in the park and every few moments he would wail, "Wait Mum, wait Mum."

But he was older now and Charlie was a gangster, and because of this he forced his legs to jog-trot endlessly in the wake of Charlie. Once he thought he heard some people shout over the other side of a little hill. He wanted to stop and listen, but Charlie strode relentlessly on. Sometimes he felt quite dizzy and was afraid he would faint, and often he felt he would give everything he had (which wasn't much) for a quiet sleep in a real bed.

Charlie spoke three times. "How do you like it up here?" he asked.

"Not much."

"Town boy, eh?" said Charlie, and Sean couldn't speak because suddenly he was overcome with a tremendous longing for the streets at home, which left him breathless.

Later Charlie said, "Not far now," and his tone was kind as though he knew how Sean felt, how dry his throat was, how his legs ached, how the thought of sausages frying was the only thing which kept him going.

They were nearly at the gully when Charlie said, "This has been a bad night for business, haven't done any at all. I daren't now, knowing people are out looking for you."

"What business? Pony killing? That's it, isn't it?" cried Sean. He stopped dead in his tracks.

Earlier moments of the day came back. The beginning of the ride with the Richardsons. The dead foal.

How could I have struck a bargain with this man just for a few sausages, he thought in horror, and now the thought of food revolted him. Tears of exhaustion came to his eyes. He thought, I can't go on. I can't go on any more.

"No. I don't kill them. They're all right, I tell you," replied Charlie, and seizing Sean he half dragged him, half carried him into the gully. "Here, sit down and rest yourself. Sleep if you like. The smell of the sausages will wake you up."

Charlie looked very rough standing over Sean, unshaven with his incongruous black shiny shoes, his dirty shirt, his general dishevelled appearance. But there was a kindness in his voice which restored Sean's confidence a little. Perhaps he isn't a killer after all. Perhaps he's a detective looking for the killers, thought Sean with a sudden rush of joy. A detective in disguise, thought Sean, because Charlie was quite unlike the detectives he had seen on TV. He looked more like one of the unsuccessful gangsters in a film Sean had seen about the underworld of London, but then wouldn't a clever detective want to look like a gangster and so go undiscovered, reasoned Sean.

"Remember, all this never happened when you get home again," said Charlie building a little fire with expert hands.

"I hope they don't find us here. Will you get into trouble if they do?" asked Sean.

"They can't prove anything," replied Charlie, striking a match, and killing all Sean's careful reasoning with that one remark.

It seemed a much longer journey back, and after a considerable time had passed Maggie realised that Jimmy was not heading towards home as she had hoped, but towards a destination which obviously appealed to him more than Mr Hill's farm.

She thought, I'm lost too now. If they've found Sean, they'll be sending out a search party for me. Oh, how tired everyone will be of the O'Connors. We'll be branded townsmen for the rest of our lives. She became unreasonably angry with Jimmy. "You're useless," she cried. "You don't take anyone home. Why didn't you take Sean back to the farm? You're a beastly pony."

She raised her hand as though to strike him, and, as he sprang back with alarmed eyes, she thought, what am I doing? What's happened to me? I nearly hit him. She said, "I'm sorry," and stroked his neck. She mounted again, gave Jimmy his head and said, "Home, home." The pony stood undecided for a moment and then started to walk determinedly in the direction he had been following ever since they left the sea.

Maggie forced him to trot. She thought, supposing Sean was in that boat? She saw him gagged, and bound. Life is terrible, she thought, full of accidents and crime. People kill foals and kidnap Sean. She had stopped using her legs and Jimmy was walking again.

"Hurry. Trot, trot I tell you, Jimmy, hurry, please, please hurry," as though he could understand.

CHAPTER ELEVEN

"Don't cry, dear. Everything will turn out all right," said Mrs Hill, trying to believe her own words.

"It's so awful. If only he was found," cried Carol, searching frantically for a handkerchief.

The two women tied Ninepin to the fence and coaxed Carol into the kitchen.

"Nothing's happened then?" asked Mrs O'Connor, while Richard buried his face in her skirt in a fit of shyness.

"No, nothing. That's what's so awful. The whole night's passed and nothing's happened. And I can't help thinking it's mostly my fault—mine and Joanna's—I can't see how we lost him. It seems so silly, he was with us one moment and the next he had vanished."

Mrs Hill pushed her gently into a chair.

"I've had breakfast," Carol said, as Mrs Hill turned towards the cooker.

"Well, he needn't have gone with you, need he?" asked Mrs O'Connor. "I shouldn't have let him go. I can see that now."

"They'll be coming back soon. They won't stay out all day," said Mrs Hill.

"I wish my husband hadn't gone. There were plenty looking without him going too," replied Mrs O'Connor.

"I expect he felt he had to."

Carol leaned back in the chair. There was something soothing about the Hills' kitchen. The clock ticked steadily, monotonously. The old dresser was hung with an assortment of china cups. It was warm and sane and welcoming, and seemed far removed from the wild moors where men and women were searching for Sean, where killers lurked as well as the wild ponies, deer and a host of birds.

But Carol couldn't stay; she didn't want to be comfortable and safe, while Sean was still lost; she wanted to act.

"Well, I must go," she cried, leaping from the chair.

"Where to, dear?" asked Mrs Hill.

"Back to the cottage. I must tell them nothing's happened. We'll have to think of something to do. The others may be back by now. Thank you," she added, out of habit, already hastening outside to untie Ninepin, to mount and wave before turning his head towards the cottage.

"She looks awful, doesn't she?—so drawn," exclaimed Mrs O'Connor.

"Carol? Yes, and she's such a good kid. We all like her," said Mrs Hill. "You won't hear a word against her in these parts."

Carol galloped Ninepin home regardless of the stones on the path. She saw that the bedroom curtains were drawn, but that the paddock and stables were empty. It meant that Joanna was home but no Mulberry unless, unless it was Sean, Sean who had been carried home injured and was now lying probably in her own bed waiting for the doctor!

Carol dismounted while Ninepin was still cantering. She threw his reins over the paddock gatepost. She rushed indoors; no dogs greeted her. Her mother was standing at the sink. She put her fingers to her lips. "Ssh," said Mrs Richardson.

"Who's upstairs?" whispered Carol. "Who is it?" Her heart was thumping against her ribs. If only Sean was found, was safe, and only suffering from a broken arm or something equally simple.

"Joanna," said Mrs Richardson.

"What's the matter with her? Where's Mulberry? Why did she come back alone? Haven't they found Sean yet?"

"Don't be so hysterical, Carol. You're too excited. Sit down and try to be sensible," said her mother.

"But Mulberry . . .?" cried Carol.

"She's lame and tied to a bush somewhere. I expect the search party will find her and bring her down."

At that moment they heard a bed creak, and Mrs Richarson said, "We've woken her up," and Joanna came into the room looking like a ghost.

"What's happening? What's all the noise about? Have they found him?" she asked.

She looked like a sleep walker standing in front of them all, half-dressed, with dark shadows under her eyes, bare feet, still half asleep.

Sylvie gave a cry of dismay. There were footsteps outside. Joanna seemed to quiver before she turned deathly pale and falling forward, fainted.

Carol cried, "She's dying," She felt she couldn't breathe; she didn't want to go on living—Joanna was dying.

Mrs Richardson was saying, "Put your head between your knees; that's right, that's fine."

Joanna's eyes opened; she pushed back her hair. Beads of sweat were on her forehead; colour came back to her cheeks.

"I'm sorry; so silly. I'm all right," she muttered.

Mr Richardson came into the room.

"Whatever's going on here?" he asked. The three dogs came after him, exhausted, their tongues hanging.

"Daddy!" cried Carol. "Is he found? Is Sean found?"

"No. Not so far as I know. I came back because I

have an important interview at eleven thirty. Others are turning back too, though not his father. I think it's a case for the police and a helicopter. What's the matter with you?" asked Mr Richardson, stopping to kiss his eldest daughter.

Police and a helicopter, thought Carol. Will they drag the bogs? She stood alone, forgotten, while everyone else fussed over Joanna. Anthony will come back soon, she thought, they're all coming back.

What does it mean? she thought. Have they given up hope? They can't have, not yet.

"We'll see to Mulberry. Now back to bed and no nonsense and your mother will bring you something to eat in a twinkling," said Mr Richardson.

They're coming back, thought Joanna, coming back; they've failed.

"They're ready. Wake up, Sean," said Charlie.

Coming back to reality Sean could only stare at Charlie; then he remembered.

"It's all right. They're not poisoned. I'm going to eat them too," said Charlie, misreading Sean's bewildered glance. He passed the tin in which the sausages had been cooked. Sean felt his mouth water. Ravenous hunger overcame all scruples; he took a sausage, swallowed it, took another and another.

"Steady on; you'd better chew them," Charlie said. It was very quiet in the gully. When Sean had devoured half the sausages, he wiped his mouth with the back of his hand, recollecting that his mother would have told him to use his handkerchief—but in Charlie's company it seemed the right thing to do.

"Thanks," he said, realising that effusive thanks would be out of place.

"Feel better?" asked Charlie.

While his companion ate, Sean had time to look round the gully. He saw the hoof-marks left earlier by Ninepin and Mulberry; the old tobacco tin, the piece of rope. It was day now, a lovely morning; it's time I found my way back, he thought. He looked again at the hoofprints.

"Have you a horse?" he asked.

"A horse? Me, a horse?" Charlie laughed. "Listen, Sean, I'm on the run. That's plain and simple, isn't it, just between you and me?"

On the run, thought Sean. What for? Good manners forbade him to ask the question. He thought, an escaped lunatic, an escaped prisoner, but from where? There's Broadmoor prison, he remembered, but he had never heard of Longmoor Prison. And why does he kill the ponies, he wondered?

"Is that why you kill the foals?" he asked.

"I don't kill them. I understand horses. I used to work with them. I catch them and a chap buys them off me."

A great weight was lifted from Sean's mind. He could let himself like Charlie a little more now. He needn't hate him now, nor regret eating his sausages.

"I'm sorry you are on the run," he said.

"Yes, it's a pity, but there it is," Charlie replied.

"How long have you been like that?"

"Nearly three years."

Sean gasped. "And the police haven't found you?"

"No, they're not so smart. I've been around a bit too, to America and back, the Continent, when things go wrong I jump on a freighter."

It seemed an exciting, improbably life to Sean.

"Did you like America?" he asked at last.

"Yes. It's tough though. I had a Cadillac for a time, but later I met with bad luck and had to sell it."

"And you came back here?"

"Yeah, I got involved in a fight; I spent a spell in jail. no-one believes an Englishman's word when it's against an American's over there," Charlie said.

Sean looked at the trees and thought, is this really happening to me? And I can't tell anyone. Not ever; I'm sworn to secrecy.

"I must get back. Mum and Dad will be in a proper state by this time," Sean said.

Charlie ignored his remark. He seemed pleased to have someone to talk to.

"I was on a ship, which was sunk on purpose, just to claim the insurance," he said.

"How awful. Can you tell me the way back, please?" asked Sean.

"Those are the only sort of jobs you can get if you're on the run. No-one respectable wants you. When they find you've no references and no proper address, they get in touch with the cops."

Sean was beginning to feel frightened again. The sausages had revived him. He longed for the safety of the caravan; to be with his parents again, Maggie and Richard. He felt he had had adventures enough to last him his life.

"I must go now," he said, standing up.

"You get tired of it after a time, every man's hand against you. No chance of steady work; only risky jobs on the wrong side of the law."

There were tears of self-pity in Charlie's eyes and Sean was more frightened than ever. He had never seen a grown man crying before. Some instinct told him to humour Charlie.

"I went through the war too; in the Falklands ..." Charlie said.

"I'm sorry. You seem to have rotten luck," Sean

replied, edging away from him, thinking, I must find my own way home, I can't stay any longer.

Then they both heard hoofs. "Lie down, don't speak," cried Charlie leaping towards him, forcing him down until he was biting damp earth.

They were riding back on two deadbeat horses. Ahead of them were other people riding back, strung out across the moors, looking like the last retreating remnants of a defeated army.

Anthony was facing reality at last. His earlier optimism had gone; he rode in silence now beside Mr Hill. They were going back to seek help, to report to the police, to appeal for help. They were the last of the expedition to turn back, and their horses were the most exhausted.

It was still morning, early morning, but by the time they were down at the farm it would be noon. They had both led their horses for mile after mile, but they found Biddy and Intruder walked faster when they were in the saddle encouraging them with legs and voice.

So twenty minutes ago they had mounted reluctantly and hadn't spoken a single word to each other since then.

He's dead. Anthony thought. It's the only answer. He must be dead. He was depressed, more depressed than he had ever been before in his whole life. They had failed and he wasn't used to failing; they were returning to the farm empty-handed, without news and without hope. They had ridden miles, driven their horses to almost complete exhaustion for a net result of nothing.

Once Anthony had thought of the foal; had Jack Dawson been round to the farm? he wondered. Had the post-mortem revealed anything? Then he thought, it won't make much difference anyway now, the killers will never return when they see the moors being combed by dogs and police.

He was worrying over Joanna when Mr Hill said, "Did you hear anything?" and stopped Biddy to listen.

Intruder stopped automatically. Anthony thought, what can he have heard? I can't hear anything. Then Intruder whinnied and there was an answering neigh and Anthony cried, "It's Mulberry. I'd know her voice anywhere." A moment later they could see her standing dejectedly tied to a bush resting her off-foreleg.

What can have happened to Joanna? thought Anthony.

"Where's her jockey?" asked Mr Hill.

They rode forward, their hearts sinking. Presently they could see that Mulberry's foreleg was twice its normal size below the knee. She whinnied again and stood with pricked ears and plaintive eyes.

"She knows her mate all right," said Mr Hill.

They dismounted. Mr Hill took the horses. Anthony went forward to Mulberry.

She nuzzled him. Her injured tendon was burning hot. Anthony thought, what can we do? How on earth shall we get her home?

"She's lame all right, isn't she?" asked Mr Hill.

"Yes, it's her tendon. She'll be lame for months," replied Anthony in a resigned voice devoid of emotion. He felt quite limp now, disheartened and rather sick.

We've been defeated all round. We haven't found Sean, or captured the killers and Mulberry's just about as lame as a horse can be. The moors have won, he thought. I suppose they always do in the end.

"I don't know what we can do; how can we get her down?" he said.

"It beats me."

"I suppose Joanna's gone on on foot," he said.

"We might get a trailer some of the way up; an open one like we use for the cows. Do you think she'd stand in that?" asked Mr Hill.

"Yes, she's wonderful to box. The best of all of ours."

The stood looking at Mulberry. Tiredness had come over Anthony quite suddenly, dulling his senses, numbing his despair for the moment.

"It means leaving her here a bit longer, that's the only thing."

" It's the only thing we can do."

They picked Mulberry some more grass.

"The sooner we get a move on the better," said Mr Hill.

They mounted their horses once more. Mulberry whinnied, pulled frantically at the bush, limped a few steps in each direction, strained against the rein which held her.

"She's terribly lame," said Anthony.

"I've seen them worse than that. It's wonderful what a horse will get over."

"But she'll never be the same again," said Anthony.

"Don't get downhearted. Everything will turn out right yet."

"It doesn't look like it."

"There's a silver lining to the darkest cloud. Maybe Sean's dodged us all and is down in the caravan now having his lunch.

"Maybe and maybe not," replied Anthony, looking

at the sky and thinking, that can't be smoke. Why should there be smoke up here? We're miles from anywhere. I must be imagining things, he thought, looking at Intruder's mane; but when he looked skywards again the smoke was still there, tantalisingly.

"That's not smoke, is it?" he asked at last.

"Smoke! Why should there be smoke? We're not home yet."

"Look in the sky. Look, it must be smoke," cried Anthony.

Mr Hill turned in his saddle. "In the sky you mean? Yes, you're right, that's smoke all right," he said.

Anthony gathered his tired wits together and picked out the landmarks he knew. Then he cried, "It's coming from the gully. It must be the killers," and suddenly his brain was crystal clear, his fatigue slid away. Here at last was hope.

"We'd better go quietly, Anthony," said Mr Hill. "Remember they may be armed."

"Yes, perhaps you're right."

"I know I am," said Mr Hill.

They turned their tired horses towards the gully, and Anthony thought, why on earth didn't we search it before, and then remembered that Joanna had taken the expedition past the gully to where she had last seen Sean.

"Looks as though we may be on to something at last," said Mr Hill.

CHAPTER TWELVE

Mrs O'Connor sat outside the farmhouse rocking backwards and forwards in an old Jacobean chair. She wished now that she had brought her knitting with her when she left the caravan; it would have soothed her nerves, and kept her hands busy; she liked to be busy and knitting passed the time. Richard was playing with a stick in the dust, drawing lines in earth which yesterday had been wet, but which was now as dry as sand.

He's dead, that's what he is, thought Mrs O'Connor for the twentieth time. Presently a car drove into the yard.

"Is Tom Hill at home?" cried Jack Dawson turning down a window.

"No," said Mrs O'Connor. "No, he isn't." She didn't feel like talking, not to anyone. She wanted to sit and unravel her thoughts, try to get things straight in her mind, to give up hoping because she couldn't bear the agony of suspense any longer.

"Mrs Hill?" Jack Dawson persisted.

But Mrs Hill appeared then.

"Hello, Jack. What's it this time?" she asked.

"Tom not at home?"

"He's up on the moors with the rest."

"Haven't they found the boy yet?"

"No, that's his mother," whispered Mrs Hill.

"Poor soul. What a mix up. What's the next move?"

"The police, I suppose."

Mrs O'Connor hadn't moved. Already she had forgotten the existence of Jack Dawson and was back on the moors imagining Sean meeting his end.

"I called about the foal. It's a good thing Tom didn't

ring up the police; the poor little beggar died of natural causes—a twisted gut. Well, that rules out foul play all right."

"Yes, no killer there," said Jack Dawson.

"What about a cup of tea? I've just made one."

"Haven't time. Thanks all the same. Muller's got a hunter lame, that big chestnut he showed last year. I hope they find the boy."

He took off his cap to Mrs O'Connor, started his car.

"Good luck. I hope they find your son all right. I shouldn't worry too much. There's not much danger on the moors at this time of year," he said before driving away.

But what about the killers? thought Mrs O'Connor.

Maggie and Jimmy reached the river and the pony went down to the edge and drank long and greedily. Wherever are we, thought Maggie? I'm sure we shouldn't be here. It was very peaceful; the river splashed calmly over boulders; woods met it on the other side and were reflected. The sun glinted on the surface of the water. Jimmy stood on green grass which he began to eat. Maggie longed to bury her face in the grass, to lie down and sleep in the sun. The river looked clean and leading Jimmy to the edge again she drank out of cupped hands.

She sat down for a moment on the bank and let her thoughts wander, imagining again how things might have been, seeing herself and Sean bathing in this very river, while their mother knitted and watched Richard and their father wrote a sonnet dedicated to the landscape, to the green wooded hills, to the dancing sunlight and of course the river.

But I must go on, she thought a moment later, I

can't give up. There can be no rest, Maggie O'Connor, until Sean is found, she thought.

"Come on, Jimmy. We've rested long enough," she said, struggling to her feet with difficulty. "Come on, move," she cried, dragging on the reins. She was weak; several minutes passed before she was able to raise Jimmy's head, to drag him away from the luscious grass down to the river edge again.

She rolled up her jeans. "Come on, we're going to cross," she said.

It was surprisingly cold in the river; the boulders were slippery; Jimmy lagged. For one awful moment Maggie thought she would never make the other side; once she slipped and nearly fell, saving herself only by hanging on to Jimmy's reins and jagging his mouth unintentionally.

When she reached the other side, it was some moments before she regained her breath.

The sight of the wooded hills disheartened her. They were steep and thick, overgrown and pathless.

But I must go on, she thought. For all I know Sean was in that boat. Time is important. If I hurry and reach a house perhaps the police can do something. They must have launches they can send out.

She began to walk up the slope dragging Jimmy. Every few strides she had to stop to marshal her strength before she could go on. She made slow progress. Jimmy continued to lag, snatched at leaves and several times stopped altogether.

And then at last she saw the outlines of a house showing through the trees. She wanted to cheer then. She tried to run, but Jimmy was still lagging and anyway her legs simply wouldn't run any more.

She thought, perhaps the people there will give me something to eat, perhaps they know about Sean, perhaps, perhaps . . . Her head started to buzz as she hurried.

She thought, supposing I never make it? Supposing I faint here among the trees? I must go on, I must go on. She could hardly see the trees now as she ran; there seemed a haze in front of her eyes, and there was a pain in her side, and her legs felt numb and stiff like sticks.

The ground was strewn with an occasional boulder, sometimes the earth was loose and seemed to slide away from under her feet; and Jimmy still lagged, dragging on her right arm and shoulder, making each step more difficult than it need have been.

Soon she could see a great deal of light shining through the trees, and presently stumbling and out of breath she reached a fence. She leaned against it, saw a paddock and beyond it a house; as she regained her breath, she realised that they were both faintly familiar, she had seen them both before.

The fence was too high for Jimmy to jump at any time, least of all in his present exhausted state; so she tied him up, climbed between the bars, and ordered her legs to cross the paddock.

As she drew near the house, her heart leapt and started to bound against her ribs. It can't be the Richardsons' cottage, she thought. She had enough strength to run, but no breath with which to call. She thought, they'll know what's happening. Perhaps Sean's found; they'll know what to do about the boat. Now suddenly she had boundless confidence in the Richardsons; she saw them picking up a telephone receiver, dialling 999, herself sitting back in a comfortable chair knowing everything was being done and that she, single-handed had uncovered a smug-

109

gling racket of foals to the Continent. She began to muddle up the sequence of events; as she ran more of her was in the cottage with the Richardsons than stumbling across the paddock. She imagined Anthony saying, "Well done, Maggie, you've found all the clues. Now we must make our final plans. What does everyone think?" Then back with herself and her aching legs, she thought she saw Carol's face at a window, and she waved her arms and gasped, "I want the police. Quick, the police." Her voice was faint, much too faint for anyone to hear. There was only another fence now and a little strip of garden between herself and the cottage. She reached the fence and saw that there really was a face at the window, and now it was smiling and calling something, and Maggie called, "I'm coming," and felt relief sweep over her, relief strong enough to bring a last rush of strength to her legs.

Joanna was asleep; Mr Richardson had gone to his appointment; Mrs Richardson and Sylvie were cooking, more to occupy their minds than anything else, since no-one felt like eating. There was nothing for Carol to do. Her tummy felt empty, but she wasn't hungry; she was tired after her short, uncomfortable sleep, but another sleep was impossible until Sean was found. Her mother had given Joanna two aspirins and Carol had begged one; but it hadn't made her feel any better and certainly it hadn't calmed her nerves. Ninepin was in the stable with plenty of hay and water and a feed. The dogs, disappointed and exhausted, just fed, were flat out, scattered about the cottage asleep. There were plenty of books to read, if Carol could have read, but that too was impossible. She was completely exhausted, but could not rest. She prowled about the cottage from one window to another, wishing that Joanna was awake and sensible, capable of relating her adventures, wishing that she was on the moors collecting poor lame Mulberry—anywhere rather than being in the cottage with nothing to do.

Her mother followed her into the sitting room.

"Do stop thumping about, you'll wake Joanna," she said.

"Sorry, I didn't know I was thumping."

"Well, you are." Everyone was in a bad temper because their nerves were on edge. Her mother went back to the kitchen. Carol collapsed in a chair, but was out of it a moment later prowling about again.

Why do things happen, she wondered? What made me ask the O'Connors to ride with us? She recalled meeting them; because of that meeting a great deal had happened; a large part of the neighbourhood had been called out to look for Sean, their arrangements had been upset; or would it have happened anyway? reasoned Carol. Was it just fate?

She halted at the sitting room window for a moment and saw someone stumbling into the paddock. Her first impulse was to call the dogs, run out and cry, "You're trespassing."

Her father hated people trespassing. He believed, 'An Englishman's home is his castle', and that that applied to his paddocks too. But she had shouted at the O'Connors yesterday and had been wrong; so now she looked again, and saw dark hair, a fringe, dirty jeans, a jersey she recognised.

She thought, is it? and looked again, before she started waving, and then calling to her mother, "Maggie's coming across the paddock without Jimmy."

She ran to the kitchen and heard Joanna calling

from the bedroom, "What is it? What's happening?" and the dull thud as she sprang out of bed.

"It's Maggie. I'm going out to meet her," she cried.

"Maggie, where's she come from?"

"She went out on Jimmy."

She opened the back door and could see Maggie plainly now, wet to the knees, stumbling like someone drunk, calling, "Dial 999. I want the police."

"We're not on the telephone. We can't. The nearest telephone is a mile and a half away."

Maggie's hopes seemed to fall in one appalling crash. Never had she imagined that the Richardsons would be without a phone.

"But I must have the police, it's urgent," she said.

"I can go on Ninepin," cried Carol. "He's terribly fast."

Mr O'Connor was turning back at last. He had missed the gully because he had been two miles on the right of it. For a long time now people had been passing him on their way home; they hadn't known what to say to Sean's father. Some of them called out, "He'll turn up presently. Don't worry too much, Mr O'Connor."

Mr Cobbett said, "Sorry I can't go on, I must get back to the farm. But the police will find him all right, you'll see."

Miss Sims said, "I'm so sorry for you. You must be going through a terrible time. You have all our sympathy."

Other people just nodded sympathetically as they passed. And to all of them Mr O'Connor said, "Thank you for your trouble."

He had meant to go on till sunset, but at noon it seemed better suddenly to turn back and seek help.

He couldn't trust other people, couldn't help thinking they might leave a stone unturned. He called Nipper who could still run as though he was out for a perfectly ordinary walk, instead of on the moors for hours.

"Come on, home, Nips. Let's go back and see what we can do," said Mr O'Connor. He knew the way back; he knew exactly how much the sun had moved since early morning, and though his watch had stopped he guessed it was noon.

He thought, what a holiday! as he turned back, and, I never want to see these moors again.

When they could see the outline of Biddy and Intruder through the trees, Charlie released Sean.

"You can get up. But remember you don't know anything. Just remember that; otherwise it'll be the worse for you." Charlie's tone was threatening because he was frightened. Sean sprang to his feet and rushed forward, calling, "Hello, I'm here." He was filled with jubilation. Already the past hours were sliding away, becoming past rather than present. He could see his parents now greeting him with open arms, welcoming him home to the caravan, perhaps even as a hero. In the joy of being found, his promises to Charlie were temporarily forgotten. He saw Biddy's plain brown head and so expected to see Maggie. "Maggie," he called, "I'm here." He reached the edge of the trees and almost collided with Anthony.

"I thought it was Maggie," he said, unable to disguise his disappointment.

He looked very small standing there, smaller than Anthony remembered him.

"Who's the chap behind you?" asked Mr Hill.

"Charlie," replied Sean and, remembering his promise, shut his mouth like a clamp.

Mr Hill took one look at Charlie, he signalled to Anthony, said something like, "This is the man we want."

Then Charlie was out of the gully on the other side, and Anthony and Mr Hill were after him urging their tired horses faster, Anthony thinking, at last, at last we've found the killer.

Sean, left behind in the gully, was half sorry for Charlie—he cooked me sausages, he thought. He said he didn't kill the ponies.

"Corner him," commanded Mr Hill.

They rode Charlie down, knocking him sideways between their horses. He lay for a moment winded, and Anthony, suddenly sorry for the man, hardened his heart, remembering the foal. Sean joined them.

"He fed me," he said. "He gave me sausages. I don't think he killed the ponies."

"Is that what he said? You can't believe a man like that—look at him—he's been living rough all night," replied Mr Hill.

And now Charlie was standing up looking like a cornered animal.

"Well, are you coming, or do you want to be knocked down again?" asked Mr Hill.

"I'll come."

"I don't think he killed the ponies. I think there's someone else in it," Sean said. Out of the corner of his eyes he could see Charlie glaring at him. He shut his mouth like a clamp again. He felt mixed up, half of him sorry for Charlie and grateful for the sausages, the other half hated him for being an outlaw, for being mixed up in the disappearance of the wild ponies.

114

"You'd better ride," said Mr Hill, pushing Sean onto Biddy's saddle.

"What's happened to Maggie?" he asked.

"She's at home looking after your mother. You've caused plenty of trouble," said Mr Hill, who was cross to find Sean able to walk and chat. "We've had the whole neighbourhood out looking for you."

"He was in pretty poor shape when I found him," Charlie said.

"Charlie gave me sausages. I've had a sleep too," Sean said. He felt in the wrong now; he had given a lot of trouble, upset the whole neighbourhood.

Anthony found the pony killer rather disappointing. He had expected there to be two men armed with guns; though Charlie looked an outlaw, he hadn't a gun, and he hadn't put up a fight, and Sean seemed on his side. Everything suddenly seemed unorthodox and unconventional to Anthony.

He said, "We'd better go down, hadn't we?"

They started to move, Mr Hill and Anthony leading their horses, Charlie between them, Sean on Biddy.

Mr Hill and Anthony were tired and it was Charlie who set the pace. Sean sitting on Biddy felt on top of the world, only at the back of his mind lurked two small worries, a sense of guilt because he had upset the neighbourhood and probably frightened his mother, and a feeling of sympathy for Charlie, which he felt shouldn't be there.

Mr Hill was thinking, nasty looking blighter. It wouldn't surprise me if he had done a spell in prison at some time or other. I'd think he was an escaped convict, if the police didn't always warn us when one was out.

"How did you get lost? Why didn't you come back, Sean?" he asked.

"Sean answered. "First of all your sister disappeared, then there was a storm. After that I fell off, then I walked miles and miles for hours and hours, until I met Charlie, who promised to tell me the way down to the farm. But I was so hungry I could hardly walk, so, he cooked me some sausages." He turned to look at Charlie; he felt he had put in a good word for him; but Charlie didn't seem to be listening; he certainly had no smile of gratitude on his face, but was striding forward, his grey eyes as hard as pebbles on a path.

"So that was it," said Mr Hill, "and we've been scouring the moors for you. I can't see how we missed you."

"He must have been in front of us all the time, and doubled back when half of us were already on our way home," said Anthony.

After that they talked no more. Except for Charlie they were exhausted. Mr Hill's heels were raw; Anthony ached all over. Sean, sitting on Biddy, dozed, reliving the last two days in his dreams.

It seemed an endless journey. I suppose whenever I come up here again I shall remember this, thought Anthony, watching Charlie walking without effort, Mr Hill limping, looking at Sean, small and unsquashable, on Biddy. I can't help liking the O'Connors, he thought, they've got so much courage.

At last they came within sight of the cottage and Anthony felt relief sweep over him. Oh for a bath, he thought.

"That's your place, isn't it?" asked Sean.

CHAPTER THIRTEEN

"My poor girl, you look exhausted. Come into the kitchen and we'll try to get things straight."

Mrs Richardson took Maggie's elbow and propelled her to a chair.

"Jimmy's tied to your fence. I found a bay and there was a boat going out. I think it takes ponies to France or somewhere. I'm afraid Sean may be on board." It all seemed improbable now, but at the time, when she had stood looking into the bay, it had seemed certain. I must convince them, she thought. "It wasn't just a fishing boat; it was big enough to take ponies. I want to tell the police," cried Maggie, who had been sitting, but now sprang to her feet.

"I'll go on Ninepin, Mum," cried Carol. Joanna had come into the room unnoticed.

"I'll go. I'm all right now," she said.

"We must find out more. It sounds like Lockspear Bay. Was it shaped like a horseshoe?" asked Mrs Richardson.

"Yes. And it had lots of rocks which you could have led ponies along and which jutted right out to sea."

"It sounds like Lockspear all right," said Joanna.

"I'll go. I'll tell the police all about it," cried Carol.

"I think they'd better come up here and talk to Maggie. They won't catch the boat anyway now," said Mrs Richardson.

"But what about Sean?" Maggie cried, standing shaking with fatigue.

"They'll know what to do," said Mrs Richardson.

Carol went to the back door. Flinging it wide she cried, "I won't be long," and then stood still, unable to believe her eyes.

"What's the matter? " cried Mrs Richardson.

They all rushed forward.

"They're coming. Look, look," screamed Carol, "And they've got Sean!"

Maggie felt completely numb with joy and relief. The nightmare was over! For she realised now it had been a nightmare.

"He's riding; so he must be all right," said Carol. Her eyes were suddenly full of tears. She'd be able to love the moors again now; Sean wouldn't haunt her for the rest of her life. They were coming towards them, nearer each moment. She started to shriek, "Hurray, hurray."

"They've got someone. Look between the two horses," said Mrs Richardson.

"They haven't got Mulberry," said Joanna.

"It must be one of the killers," cried Carol running out into the sunshine.

Sylvie, who had been for a walk and missed everything, joined them now.

"What happens?" she cried.

Poor Mulberry, thought Joanna.

He's safe, thought Maggie, beginning to wave and stagger after Carol on stiff legs.

"If they have one of the killers, Sean will not have been lost in vain," said Mrs Richardson.

"Hello," cried Anthony.

Mr Hill waved his cap above his head. Sean shouted, "I'm all right. I was lost."

Maggie stood still and waited for them. Carol ran on, Joanna called, "Did you see Mulberry?"

Presently they were all together, talking, explaining, laughing. Only Mr Hill and Charlie stood aloof, watching one another.

"I fell off. Jimmy shied," explained Sean.

"I've been miles and miles looking for you. I took Jimmy. Mr Hill will probably be furious when he knows," said Maggie. Mrs Hill said it didn't matter. She told me you had," replied Carol.

"He's something to do with the pony killers; but I don't think he killed them," Sean whispered to Maggie, who passed it on to the Richardsons.

"All I want is a bath!" exclaimed Anthony.

"What about this fellow?" asked Mr Hill.

Yes, what about him, Anthony wondered. Where do we go from here?

"I'll go for the police. I'm not tired, nor's Ninepin," cried Carol, and no-one could stop her now. In a moment she was putting a headcollar on Ninepin, vaulting on him, galloping away, determined at least to have a share in the capture of the pony killer.

"I'll take Biddy and Intruder to the stable," said Joanna, "they look exhausted."

"The rest of you had better come in and have something to eat," said Mrs Richardson, who was wishing her husband was at home to help. "Come on, don't stand dithering," she said sharply, because no-one had moved.

Her words had the right effect. They followed her into the kitchen and all sat down, Mr Hill and Anthony each on one side of Charlie.

"Would someone mind shutting the windows?" asked Anthony.

It's like a gangster film, thought Maggie, helping to bolt the back door.

Poor Charlie, he's caught now, thought Sean. Any moment and the police will be here.

I mustn't fall asleep, thought Anthony. In about twenty minutes the police will be here and then I shall be able to have a bath and sleep and sleep.

"Joanna cannot get in," Sylvie.

Maggie let Joanna in.

"I've fed them. What about Mulberry?" asked Joanna.

"I'll see about getting her down. She won't hurt for the time being," replied Mr Hill.

"I'll collect Jimmy. Someone lock the door after me," said Joanna.

Everything seemed like a dream now to Maggie. She leaned back in her chair and saw again the bay and the boat going out. Mrs Richardson passed round cups of tea and sandwiches.

"There'll be something more substantial in a moment," she said.

Sylvie was cooking omelettes. Charlie made polite conversation. "Nice kitchen you have here," he told Mrs Richardson. "Where do you come from?" he asked Sylvie.

Who is he? wondered Joanna. Where does he come from? It's over, thought Sean, but what a story I shall have to tell, and now Charlie is caught I can tell it.

Some time later, when the police had still to arrive, and everyone had been fed, there was a knock on the door and when Maggie and Joanna had undone the bolts, Mr O'Connor was standing on the threshold framed by the afternoon sun.

"No-one's had any news of my son then?" he asked.

"He's here," cried Maggie.

"Dad!" shrieked Sean.

Standing there he looked like someone from another world. His eyes seemed to look without seeing, so heavy was his tiredness. His dark hair stood on end like a halo. His boots were heavy with mud; his hands hung straight and limp.

"Here?" he said.

But now Sean had his right hand, so there could be no mistake.

"Yes, here, Dad," he cried.

"I've told Mrs O'Connor and she's coming up with Richard," said Carol.

"So there's nothing to worry about. Sit down and join the party," said Mrs Richardson.

Sean led his father to a chair and Mr O'Connor looked at Maggie and said, "What are you doing here? I thought you were stopping with your mother."

Joanna was bolting the door and then they all heard footsteps coming up the path and it was the police.

Charlie seemed to grow smaller when he heard them coming in. He stood up, walked across the room to Sean and said, "Goodbye, all the best."

A lump rose in Sean's throat as he shook the offered hand. He was ashamed now that he had looked forward to telling the boys at home about Charlie. He looked at the ground, because he didn't want anyone to see the anguish in his face. He said, "Goodbye and all the best." He felt that everyone was looking at him, surprised to see him shaking a criminal by the hand. But they've got no proof, no proof at all, he thought.

"I'd like some statements, please," said the policeman in the peaked cap.

"You'll have to wait for them. Can't you see everyone is exhausted?" said Mrs Richardson.

"Later," said Mr O'Connor. "Sean is a minor. You can't have a statement from him without my consent."

If they hadn't thought Charlie killed wild ponies,

at that moment their sympathy would probably have been with him. As it was, they all wanted time in which to collect their wits, to calm their exhausted nerves.

At last the police went and Mrs O'Connor appeared carrying Richard.

"So here you are, you little monkey," she cried running to Sean, showering him with kisses. "And we've been worried stiff, you naughty boy," she cried.

"I'd best be going. Biddy and Jimmy should be rested by now," said Mr Hill.

"I can't thank you enough," said Mr O'Connor coming to life suddenly.

"You couldn't have done more," cried Mrs O'Connor and for a moment everybody thought she was going to kiss Mr Hill on the cheek.

"I'll help you off," said Joanna.

"It was nothing," said Mr Hill.

The money. We haven't paid him for the horses, thought Maggie. She hurried after Mr Hill.

"How much do we owe you?" she asked. She felt herself blushing as she stood there waiting for a reply.

"Owe me? What, for hiring the horses? Why, nothing. Forget it," said Mr Hill striding away, a square figure in the evening light.

Presently, when there was at last a silence, Mrs O'Connor said, "I think we'd best be going down now, to be cooking and everything."

Why don't you stay here tonight? There's plenty of room. I've got several extra put-up beds and there's the sofa," said Mrs Richardson. "It's late to be going down now, and cooking and supper."

The O'Connors stood undecided.

"Yes, stay," shrieked Carol. Maggie can sleep in our room, can't she Mum?"

"That's a great idea," said Joanna.

Mrs O'Connor tried to argue. "It's putting you to so much trouble, and then Richard may wake you all up in the middle of the night."

"We're used to that. Anyway my kids were babies once," said Mrs Richardson.

So in the end they stayed.

Maggie slept, but later when she wakened and saw that there was moonlight in the room she realised that Carol was watching her.

"I hoped you'd wake up," Carol said.

"I can't help thinking what a nuisance we've been; everyone must loathe the name of O'Connor now. I don't suppose Mr Hill will ever let us have Biddy and Jimmy again and I can't blame him either," said Maggie. It was the hour when everything seems blackest, and now that the anxiety and suspense were over and she had rested, Maggie thought she could see everything in proper perspective.

"But it was our fault—Joanna's and mine. Everybody knows that and, if they don't, I'll soon tell them. We were supposed to look after Sean, you know we were." In her agitation Carol sat up and her duvet slid to the floor.

"Whatever's going on?" asked Joanna.

"And anyway if Mr Hill won't let you have his horses, you can come up here and ride Ninepin in the paddock. We can all teach each other."

"That would be great," said Maggie. "I know we're terrible riders."

"I think you're fine. You can't help it if you haven't ridden much."

"Do go to sleep. You'll wake Sylvie," said Joanna.

123

Sean watched the stars. At last he couldn't stop himself saying, "I've been an real nuisance, haven't I. But at any rate we've caught Charlie."

"Where do you think he is now?"

"I think he's innocent."

"Then he'll be let off."

Sean lay in bed worrying about Charlie. Anthony drifted back to sleep.

In the morning they all went down to the police station in some trepidation. Sean was remembering his promises to Charlie. Were they still valid, he wondered? They were all still tired. Mulberry had been brought home by Mr and Mrs Richardson in Mr Hill's open trailer by the light of the moon. She stood in the stable looking very sorry for herself. The other horses were all resting. The day was perfect and the moors looked kind and peaceful.

They all walked as far the garage and then piled into the Richardsons' car.

"I can't see that we've got a shred of evidence on which the police can convict the man," said Mr Richardson, starting his car.

"Perhaps he's left his fingerprints on something," suggested Anthony.

"But on what? The foal died a natural death. The man's obviously guilty but there's no evidence."

No-one felt like arguing with Mr Richardson. Sean could have said a lot, but he was afraid of him; he reminded him of Councillors who visited his school, and of one in particular who gave away the prizes.

They were ushered into the police station by a constable. "The Superintendent will see you in a moment," he said.

Sylvie, Mrs Richardson, Mrs O'Connor and Richard had stayed outside in the cars.

"It's not very big," cried Sean.

"But this isn't all of it," said Carol.

Presently Mr O'Connor and Mr Richardson were taken in to see the Superintendent.

"This is worse than waiting to go into a show ring," said Joanna.

"I wish they'd hurry up," exclaimed Maggie.

"What do you think they'll want to know?" asked Sean.

"Only a statement of what you were doing yesterday," replied Anthony.

Presently the fathers came out.

"Maggie first," said Mr Richardson.

"They want to know more about the boat," said Mr O'Connor.

Each in turn, the children made a statement. Before Sean went in, Mr O'Connor seemed to read his thoughts. "Whatever you say won't make any difference to Charlie," he said.

Afterwards, when it was over and the constable had ushered them out, Mr Richardson said, "How about some coffee and an explanation? What do you say, Mr O'Connor?"

"Just right," agreed Mr O'Connor.

When they were sitting in a large restaurant, Mr Richardson started to explain.

Charlie went absent from the army, after he was caught taking drugs about three years ago. He has been on the run ever since knowing that if he was caught he would be court-martialled.

"But what about the ponies?" cried Carol.

"Wait a moment. I'm coming to that," said Mr Richardson.

125

By this time ices and cakes, milk shakes and coffee had started to arrive, so for a minute or two conversation stopped. Then Mr Richardson resumed.

"As for the ponies, he doesn't appear to know what happened to them. He merely handed them over to two men he met outside a pub three weeks ago whom he knew as Percy and Bill. He was finding it increasingly difficult to catch any ponies, having started with the tame ones and any foals he could get near."

"Altogether it must have been a pretty strange set-up," said Mr O'Connor.

"Percy and Bill are probably the men in the boat Maggie saw. They are believed to ship the ponies straight to France alive, where they fetch good prices," continued Mr Richardson.

"Ugh, how horrible," cried Carol.

After that there didn't seem much more to tell. The police had already expressed their gratitude to the children, and warned Sean not to get lost again as he might not be so lucky a second time.

"I'm so glad Charlie's not really guilty," said Sean.

"You'll never get over those sausages, will you?" asked Anthony.

"Maggie and Sean are going to ride Ninepin tomorrow in the paddock. You don't mind, do you. Mr O'Connor?" asked Carol.

"Not as long as they stop in the paddock. I don't want them riding on the moors again," replied Mr O'Connor.

"Maggie can have Intruder if she likes," offered Anthony.

"We're going to school one another," Carol said.

"We're going to learn to ride properly, Dad," Maggie said.

When the bill was paid they went back to the cars.

"We'll drop you off at the farm." said Mr Richardson.

And as they drove away from the town towards the moors again, Maggie could only think, somehow everything's turned out all right after all. She saw the days ahead filled with lessons in the paddock. Soon we'll really be able to ride, she thought.

"I'm glad Charlie's not really guilty," said Sean again. "I suppose we'll all be in the papers soon."

"If I know anything about reporters the place will be swarming with them by this afternoon," replied Mrs Richardson.

Climbing out of the cars, waving goodbye, Maggie and Sean thought with one accord, they're not a bit stuck up after all, and this is going to be the best holiday of all.

Carol said, "I like the O'Connors. Isn't it terrible now, that we hated them coming?"

"It shows how wrong one can be," said Anthony.

"I thought they'd be awful tourists," said Joanna.

"But everyone's a tourist sometime. We are when we go to France," said Mrs Richardson.

True to Mrs Richardson's expectations, by twelve o'clock reporters were interviewing the O'Connors and Richardsons. Next morning papers were plastered with their photographs. Three months later, when Percy John Atterson of no fixed address, and Henry Albert Jones of Stepney, London were charged with unlawfully exporting live ponies to France, their photographs were to be seen again.